NO PRISONERS

Skye Fargo heard a sound, and he spun, crouching, as he drew his Colt.

His Ovaro was making the noise. Fargo saw a hand grabbing the saddle horn, and a foot below the horse's belly.

Fargo sprinted to his right, hoping to get a shot. A mat of wet oak leaves slid beneath his boots, and he fought for his balance.

The Ovaro was almost into the trees, but the thief's back stuck out. It was now or never.

There were some things a man couldn't take lightly. Fargo shot to kill.

The Trailsman had left civilization far behind . . . in a wilderness filled with wild boars, marauding bears, deadly Comanches, and a mysterious enemy more dangerous than all of them combined. . . .

TEXAS HELL COUNTRY

by

Jon Sharpe

Ⓞ
A SIGNET BOOK
NEW AMERICAN LIBRARY

PUBLISHER'S NOTE

This book is a work of fiction. Names, characters, places, and incidents either are the product of the author's imagination or are used fictitiously, and any resemblance to actual persons, living or dead, events, or locales is entirely coincidental.

Copyright © 1988 by Jon Sharpe

The first chapter of this book previously appeared in *Call of the White Wolf,* the eighty-fifth book in this series.

SIGNET TRADEMARK REG. U.S. PAT. OFF. AND FOREIGN COUNTRIES
REGISTERED TRADEMARK—MARCA REGISTRADA
HECHO EN DRESDEN, TN, USA

SIGNET, SIGNET CLASSIC, MENTOR, ONYX, PLUME, MERIDIAN
and NAL BOOKS are published by NAL PENGUIN INC.,
1633 Broadway, New York, New York 10019

First Printing, February, 1989

1 2 3 4 5 6 7 8 9

PRINTED IN THE UNITED STATES OF AMERICA

The Trailsman

Beginnings . . . they bend the tree and they mark the man. Skye Fargo was born when he was eighteen. Terror was his midwife, vengeance his first cry. Killing spawned Skye Fargo, ruthless, cold-blooded murder. Out of the acrid smoke of gunpowder still hanging in the air, he rose, cried out a promise never forgotten.

The Trailsman, they began to call him, all across the West: searcher, scout, hunter, the man who could see where others only looked, his skills for hire but not his soul, the man who lived each day to the fullest, yet trailed each tomorrow. Skye Fargo, the Trailsman, the seeker who could take the wildness of a land and the wanting of a woman and make them his own.

*The Texas Hill Country, a few days
before Christmas, 1859—where
the forests are teeming with
wild pigs, hungry bears,
and desperate men . . .*

1

The bushy evergreen really didn't have a chance. For starters, the tree wasn't much taller than either of the big men standing before it. Likely they could have just pushed hard and toppled it, but the men were taking turns with a broadax as the December sun began to sag low toward the hill country of central Texas.

"These goddamn cedars are so bushy near the trunk that it's a day's work just to reach in there with an ax blade." Green-eyed, red-bearded, and built as stout as a bulldog, Thomas Jefferson Baker took another whack. A hand-sized chip flew out, struck a low branch, and dropped into the thin, stony soil.

"Should have brought a saw, I reckon. Then we could cut off some of the lower limbs and get in there and chop this down before it gets too dark." Taller than Baker but not as husky, black-bearded Skye Fargo took the ax and swung. The tree shuddered.

"If we was just clearin' some land, that'd be the way to do it," Baker agreed. "But we want this one as bushy as we can keep it. Greta'd never forgive me if we came back to the house with an ugly hacked-up Christmas tree."

Fargo nodded while making sure that the fringed buckskin jacket he'd shed was still close by, draped over a stump. It was a pure pleasure to be outdoors a couple days before Christmas and not need to wear much more than a flannel shirt. He'd finally made it south in time to enjoy a mild Texas winter.

"Yeah, that juniper ought to make a handsome tree once Greta strings it with popcorn and puts a few candles on it."

Baker finished his swing before turning to Fargo.

"Long as I've known you, Skye, I know better'n to call you a liar. But why for are you calling this a juniper? Everybody knows it's just a cedar."

Fargo took his own swing, and the tree began to topple as the men stepped back. "Tom, you can call it whatever you want to call it. You Texans seem to do things pretty much your own way, no matter what anybody else does. But the fact is, that's a Mexican juniper, not a cedar."

Baker turned to face the Trailsman. "Hell, cedar's all I ever heard 'em called."

"Sniff one of the chips, Tom," Fargo replied. "It won't smell like a cedar chest. Besides, see those little blue berries? Crush one and take a whiff. Smells just like English gin, which stands to reason because they use juniper berries for flavor."

Baker scooped up a chip and some berries. "I'll be damned, Skye. You're right. But it sure looks like a real cedar, what with those little green web leaves."

Fargo nodded. "Really can't blame folks for calling those junipers cedars, even if real cedars don't grow hereabouts." He paused. "What's next? Drag this back to your house so Greta can start to work on it?"

"Got another hour or so of light," Baker said, "so we don't exactly need to rush ourselves." He picked up a piece of grass rope, about twenty feet long, and tied it to the base of the downed tree.

As the two old friends caught up on each other, they strolled leisurely, tree in tow, toward Baker's farmstead, over on the other side of a small rise in this rolling timbered country.

Tom Baker had been surprised as hell to see Skye Fargo, the Trailsman, earlier this afternoon. Just as the farmer was stepping out of his substantial log barn, ax in hand for fetching a Christmas tree, up rode a tall man, muscled but whipcord-lean. He sat easily astride an Ovaro pinto stallion whose gleaming white midsection was framed by jet-black fore- and hindquarters.

As soon as Baker recognized him, Fargo was invited to put the Ovaro in a stall in the barn, and he joined Tom Baker on the jaunt to fetch a Christmas tree.

Skye Fargo had been heading south and west, down

from Missouri after some business near Kansas City. After more than a month of tense riding through Indian country, the comfortable, almost luxurious, Nimitz Hotel in Fredericksburg seemed as good a place as any to lay up for a couple days. Most of the local talk was in the guttural native speech of the German emigrants who populated this part of Texas, but he heard enough English to put two and two together.

It seemed that about seven years before, Greta Gottlieb, the beautiful blond daughter of a prosperous hardware merchant in San Antonio, had shocked everyone by marrying a red-bearded American, rather than a fellow German. And when Fargo discovered that the groom was named Baker, he made inquiries about finding the couple at the farm that they were carving out of the rock-strewn countryside.

The Trailsman carried fond memories of Greta. Her relatives and neighbors would doubtless be a lot more shocked if they had known just how warm-natured she had been back when Fargo had first met her during a fiesta down in San Antonio. Greta Gottlieb, though, had wanted to settle down and raise a family with a strong, hardworking man. Skye Fargo was as strong as they came, and he never backed off from work that had to be done, but he was the kind of man who'd never settle down, even with a woman like Greta.

In those days, Tom Baker wasn't exactly the settling type, either. He and the Trailsman had ridden together on one of the meanest jobs in the West. The Butterfield Stage Line generally carried the U.S. mail and up to a dozen uncomfortable passengers for thirteen hundred miles between San Antonio, Texas, and San Diego, California. The sunbaked desert trip took four weeks that seemed like eternity. On account of the Comanche and Apache, each trip required six armed escorts.

For a few months, Fargo and Tom Baker had been among those forty-dollar-a-month escorts. One blistering morning in San Diego, Fargo had been offered other work, trailing Mexican cattle north to San Francisco. He took it. Tom Baker had figured it was time to quit, too. But he made one last run, back to San

Antonio, a town he liked, and the two men hadn't seen each other since then.

"So they call you the Trailsman now?" Baker asked as they neared the house, its windows glowing in the twilight.

"Among other things." Fargo chuckled as they swung to their right to avoid dragging a tree through Greta's dormant garden. "Looks like you're doing well for yourself here."

Like many Texas houses, this one was built of logs, although it was chinked more tightly than most. The homestead was really two structures that sat a few paces apart. They were connected by a covered walkway that inspired folks to call these "dogtrot houses." Baker's had grown some recently with a new lean-to on one side. That must be where they'd put the kitchen, since blue-gray smoke rose from the stone chimney.

"Can't complain," Baker said. "Clear a little more land every year. Raise a few cattle, run a few hogs, grow some corn and this and that, and we get by."

"More than get by," Fargo said, noting a quick-moving low silhouette pass a window. "Either you've got a trick dog that walks on its hind legs, or you and Greta have a family now."

Even in the near-darkness, Baker's smile showed. "That little hellion is William Barret Travis Baker. He just turned six."

"So you named your son after the commander at the Alamo," Fargo commented. "That's sure a mouthful for a name, but I suppose when you go Texas, you go all the way."

"Something like that," Baker said and chuckled. "We just call him Billy, though, unless he's in trouble. Which happens often enough." Only steps from the door, the husky man halted.

So did Fargo. There was a muted crackle, followed by rustling in the trees, about a hundred yards off, back the way they'd just come. Fargo's hand dropped to the heavy army-model Colt revolver that never left his side. He started to crouch and felt Baker's hand on his shoulder.

"It's too dark, Skye. And like as not, it don't mean nothin'."

Fargo straightened. "Happen before?"

"You hear brush sounds out here all the time. Lately things have been a little spooky, though. Remember how it was that night before the Apache attacked us on the other side of El Paso? Had that feeling you were being watched, but you couldn't put your finger on anything?"

Fargo muttered agreement.

"That's how this has been for the past couple months. Get that feeling every now and again, but there never seems to be anything to it."

"Nosy neighbors, maybe?"

"We're the only house for four or five miles any which way," Baker explained. "Maybe it's just wild pigs in the brush."

"Javelinas are either real noisy or they don't make any sound," Fargo grunted. "Sounded two-legged to me."

"Well, you've got folks moving through here that're trying to stay hidden. Slaves that manage to escape from the cotton plantations to the east sometimes come through here, sneaking their way to Mexico, where they'll be free."

Fargo nodded. That made sense. Considering the substantial bounties of two or three hundred dollars that were posted on escaped slaves, a fugitive wouldn't be likely to cause any trouble. He'd just want to stay hidden. But still, it was irksome to see how Tom Baker, once so curious and adventuresome, was getting so settled these days that he wouldn't even investigate strange noises near his house.

"Talk to the local law about this?" Fargo wondered.

"Isn't any worth mention. There's a sheriff over to Fredericksburg, but he don't get out this way much."

"Texas Rangers?"

"They'd take care of it, for sure. But the Comanche are fractious to the north and west, out along the frontier, so that's where all the Rangers are."

"Could it be Comanche in your brush? Don't they still roam hereabouts?"

"Not enough to matter. When the Germans started to settle hereabouts, back before our time here—it'd be '47, I reckon—their head man, John Meusebach, made a deal with the Penatka Comanche. Both sides have held to it pretty good. Comanche don't get along so good with the rest of Texas, but we manage here."

Obviously tired of speculating, Baker started moving again, toward the long front porch of his dogtrot house. After they set the tree on the porch, they stepped inside.

Fargo didn't quite know which felt better—the smell of a decent meal, or the way that tiny Greta nearly toppled him with a long embrace for an old friend.

"Skye, Skye, I can't believe it is really you. What a Christmas present to have you visit us." Her long golden hair was done up in braids that she had pinned around atop her head, and she wore a patched and splattered apron that nearly reached the scrubbed plank floor. Since he'd last seen her, she had added a few pounds, mostly in the right places. Greta still looked and felt mighty good.

Seeing as she was now a married woman with her husband and son beside her, the Trailsman tried to ignore the stirring that came when Greta's ample bosom pressed against his abdomen as she nestled her head against his chest for a moment.

Besides, Fargo had other desires. At the moment, the Trailsman felt hungry enough to skin a dead skunk and start chewing. Greta returned to the cast-iron cook stove in the back room. Fargo found a chair, its seat covered with tanned deer hide, and relaxed. He leaned back, savoring the pungent aroma of spicy sausage frying with potatoes.

Most everywhere else in the Lone Star State, meals consisted of greasy bacon and chunky corn pone—breakfast, dinner, and supper. Even though Texans considered pecans fit for hog feed and not much else, Fargo had found the nuts a welcome relief from the state's usual fare. And a cheap one, since pecan trees were almost as common as the "cedars."

Little Billy started to disturb the Trailsman's comfortable languor, but his father shushed him after only a few chatters. General silence continued through the hearty dinner. Once Greta had hauled the plates away, though, everyone opened up, especially when she brought out a bottle of wine that a neighbor had put up from local wild grapes.

Billy seemed impressed by the tall visitor, although his face fell when he learned that Skye Fargo was not a Texas Ranger.

"But you know Rangers, don't you?" the boy asked.

Fargo smiled. Billy had his dad's red hair and stocky build, with his mother's chin, nose, and mouth. "Sure, Billy, I know a few Rangers. Even rode with them a time or two."

"Really?"

Fargo told a few tales without stretching the truth much, about what he'd been doing the past few years.

"Won't you ever settle down?" Greta wondered.

"The day may come," Fargo granted. "And a man could do a lot worse than what you folks have managed. But there's things that gnaw at a man and just won't let him rest."

Tom and Greta's eyes met Fargo's. They knew his past. When not much more than a boy, Skye Fargo had visited away from home—a remote Wells Fargo stage station run by his father. During his absence, two raiding men had burned the station and butchered the family. The young man who returned to the ruins and the slaughter changed his name to Skye Fargo and vowed to search for the culprits. Until he found them and dealt them justice, he couldn't ever settle.

There was no sense discussing that in front of the boy, so Greta changed the subject.

"Billy, it is time for bed."

Tom stifled a yawn and added, "In fact, it's time for all of us to get some shut-eye. There's plenty to do tomorrow."

With doleful eyes, the boy examined the ladder that led upstairs to the loft above the main room.

"Please, Mama, can't I stay up and listen to more of Mr. Fargo's stories?"

She shook her head. "No. Maybe tomorrow."

If the boy had moved any slower, he'd have been going backward, but eventually he got up to the loft.

"What's the plan here?" Fargo wondered aloud. "I can bring in my bedroll and bunk up there with him."

Tom looked relieved as Greta nodded and said that would be fine.

"Before I bed down, though, I want to borrow a lantern," the Trailsman said. "Finding my bedroll and the rest of my possibles in an unfamiliar barn could be tricky in the dark. Besides, I just recalled that I left my jacket where we cut the tree."

"I can come along and show you the way." Tom rose to fetch a coal-oil lantern.

"No, I can handle it fine." Fargo got up and beat his host to the lantern. He turned and winked. "Best you not waste any time getting into bed."

Tom Baker sported a ruddy complexion anyway, and the waving orange light from the room's only lamp reddened him. So it was hard to be sure whether the man was blushing. "Yep," he finally said. "Bed does sound a sight more comfortable than fetching that jacket. See you in the morning, Skye."

The jacket was simply an excuse to get out of the house for a spell. Fargo could almost feel the tension inside. Something wasn't sitting right with Tom Baker.

Maybe it was the prowlers or whatever he had been sensing that made him seem edgy. More likely, it was the presence of Skye Fargo, a man who had spent considerable time around Greta back when he was in and out of San Antonio on a regular basis.

That liaison was long past over. Fargo and Greta were friends and nothing more these days. But no man Fargo knew—and the Trailsman didn't think that if the time came he'd be an exception—ever felt entirely comfortable around any other man who'd once been close to his wife.

So he and Tom Baker would both likely feel better if the Trailsman rode on tomorrow. Fargo could reach New Braunfels easily, maybe even San Antonio. It wouldn't be the first Christmas he'd spent alone and moving on. Visiting old friends had seemed like such a good idea yesterday. He and Tom had once been as close as brothers, but a lot had gone by since then. As much as it sometimes pained you, you just had to let it go by.

Guided by starlight and a sliver of a moon, Fargo found the buckskin jacket quickly enough. He didn't light the lantern until his return trip, when he reached the general area where those rustling and crackling sounds had come from earlier.

Under a moss-ridden post oak, the Trailsman found human tracks. They didn't stand to reason. An escaping slave would likely be going barefoot, even in December. Comanches wore moccasins. The impressions, barely visible in the thin soil, had been formed by boots. But the heels spread too wide and the toes ran too broad to be the boots worn by Texans. Something like army boots, from the look of them.

Further study showed that there were two men in such boots that had been lurking there this afternoon. Their perch gave them a good view of the dogtrot cabin while allowing the men to stay out of sight behind some brush. From the length of their paces, Fargo judged that the men had been about the same height and weight—about five-eight and one hundred sixty pounds. Just about average, both of them.

Tracking them was an appealing notion, but not a very smart one. Without the lantern, even the Trailsman's keen eyes wouldn't find their trail. With it lit, he was an easy target if he should get close to them. The pursuit would have to wait till morning. Not that they'd done anything except snoop, which was suspicious, but hardly a crime. Maybe it wasn't even a threat, or worth worrying about.

Even so, Fargo's curiosity was inspired. He sure didn't have anything better to do when he rode out tomorrow.

The next day seemed to arrive too early. Fargo was still tired, wanting nothing more than to go back to snoring and dreaming. And the exuberant Billy started pestering the Trailsman with questions as soon as there was light. Fargo tried hard to keep his eyes closed and ignore the disturbance, but it was a lost cause.

Yes, he had killed some "Injuns." Even back when he'd been riding with Billy's pa. Giving up any hope of rest, Fargo gave the boy a detailed account of an Apache attack on the mail coach, one blistering day near Tucson. Then came scores of questions about California, Oregon, Kansas, and the remote Rocky Mountains.

"Gee, you've been everywhere and done everything. And my pa . . ."

"Your dad got around plenty before he decided to settle down," Fargo explained. "Best you don't hold it against him if his life doesn't sound quite as exciting as mine."

"But all he does is tend to crops and critters," the boy protested. "You're a real hero."

"Billy, likely you're too young to understand. Lots of boys get to be grown men, and they never understand. But the real heroes in Texas and everywhere else in the West are folks like your ma and pa. They just settle in and do a lot of thankless hard work, day in and day out. My life's easy compared to theirs. And when something bad comes up, your folks and people like them show how much sand they have. They fight for what's theirs and for what's right."

Although talking reason to a six-year-old was generally impossible, Fargo could see that the kid was paying heed. So he continued. "Besides all that, if your pa was still off fighting Comanche and Apache to the west, do you think he could have married up and had a little boy named William Barret Travis Baker?"

The kid looked thoughtful. "Nope. I reckon not." He reached for some clothes, pulled them on, and headed down the ladder. Fargo followed a couple of minutes later.

Greta was already stirring griddle cakes. Made with real wheat flour, rather than the customary Texas cornmeal, the flapjacks tasted like manna to the Trailsman. During the mealtime silence, Fargo gazed out the window.

This homestead came close to being self-sufficient. He spotted the henhouse and its yard. Nearby sat the smokehouse, the source of homemade sausages and hams. A path, leading to the log barn and the privy, veered off to the right.

Around the chicken yard and hog pen were rail fences, different from the usual. Everywhere else, the fence rails were stacked in zigzags. Here, they ran straight, held up by posts that sat in pairs, just far enough apart for the rails, bound together at the top with rawhide. It was a way to build a solid fence without the labor of stone or the expense of nails, which had to be imported from the East.

While they sipped coffee afterward, Fargo got Tom Baker to brag some on his place. "It's been a powerful lot of work. And it seems like I'm always tryin' something different. If I ain't making fence, I'm nursing sick pigs. And if I ain't laying a stone foundation, I'm making shoes."

He paused. "Getting to be a tolerable cobbler, though." He laughed. "Don't know about the rest, but I can generally cobble something together when I need to."

"Looks to me like you manage to figure it out pretty well as you go along," Fargo responded. "You've got a lot to be proud of here, Tom."

Baker smiled. "You can't know how glad I am to hear you say that, Skye."

"Didn't hurt me a bit to say it, but what makes you so blessed glad about it?"

Baker hemmed and hawed for a bit. "Guess I was worried when you rode up yesterday, Skye."

"Worried? About what?"

"Oh, here I am, stuck on a little farm in the middle of nowhere, bein' a nobody. And hell, every time I get down to San Antonio and wander into a saloon, there's folks tellin' stories about the famous Trailsman. Ain't nobody believes me when I say I used to ride with that esteemed gent. It hurts sometimes."

"It would," Fargo agreed. "But you're building something good and lasting here. Something I'll likely never enjoy. We went different ways that morning in San Diego, but I can't see that you've got cause for regret. You always rode hard and shot straight and saw clear. It could have just as easy turned out that those saloon idlers would be telling tall tales about Thomas Jefferson Baker."

Greta appeared with more coffee. "Maybe so," Baker agreed after a steaming sip. "How long you fixing to stay, Skye? You better know you're welcome."

"Likely I'll move on today. Christmas is in just a couple days, and that's a family day."

"Hell, Skye, you come as close to family as anybody I ever had before I got married. I was orphaned too, you recall. So stick around."

Fargo mulled on that while holding his cup. Finally he lifted it to his lips and took a healthy swallow. "Suppose I could, at that. But I hate to just sit around, not earning my keep. And this is a farm."

"So?"

"So what I know about farming could be stuck inside a thimble, and it'd still hold a thimbleful of water. I'd likely spook your cow dry the first time I tried to milk her. I never herded hogs, and I'm not much of a hand with fences. You find me some chores where I won't do more harm than good, and I'll stick around for the holiday."

Greta came into the front room from the kitchen just then. "I know what he can do."

Fargo sincerely hoped the pigsty didn't need to be shoveled out.

"Kristina," Greta continued. "Someone needs to get her at the Sunday house."

"That's a perfect chore for the Trailsman," Baker agreed. He turned to Fargo. "Kristina is Greta's kid sister. Their parents live in San Antonio—but you knew that, didn't you?"

"Herr Ludwig has a big hardware store on Commerce Street, if I remember right," Fargo replied. "There was a brother, too, wasn't there?"

"Paul. He went back to the old country last year. Anyway, the folks don't feel up to traveling. And with our livestock and no neighbors close by, we couldn't get away for the week or so it would take to get to San Antonio and back. So that Greta can be with some of her family on the holiday, Kristina is coming to visit us."

"What's this about a Sunday house?" Fargo wondered aloud.

"I'll get to that." Baker set his coffee cup down. "She's taking the stage and gets to Fredericksburg today. She'll stay at our Sunday house until we get in there and bring her out to the homestead."

"I'd be proud to ride over to Fredericksburg and escort her back here," Fargo replied. "But how do I find this Sunday house?"

Baker's curly beard shook as he smiled. "Sorry, Skye, I forgot you're not from hereabouts. Most of us with farms in the hill country do our trading and go to church in Fredericksburg. So we need to stay over there on Saturday and Sunday."

Fargo interrupted him. "When I was through there, I saw a lot of little houses made out of local limestone. They looked empty. Those'd be the houses you folks use when you're visiting town on Sunday—your Sunday houses?"

The farmer nodded. "Go to the head of the class, Skye." He gave directions for his Sunday house, a couple of blocks off Fredericksburg's main street, and Fargo was soon on his way.

2

Otto Friedrich, the bald and egg-shaped gent who manned the Fredericksburg end of the San Antonio & Northern Express Line, again consulted his pocket watch.

"I can't say, why the coach is so late, Mr. Fargo. It's always here by two o'clock, unless there's a flood. Perhaps the road is muddier than usual."

Fargo thanked the man, more out of politeness than sincerity. Then he stepped outside so that he could pace around on a dirt street rather than a plank floor. He didn't really see why the station agent was already acting so concerned about Kristina's stage running late.

It was only half-past two, and most stage lines in the West ran on fairly casual schedules. Thirty minutes one way or the other never meant all that much to anybody except these Germans, who seemed to take punctuality as seriously as they took cleanliness.

But after the Trailsman had ridden into town and come up empty at the Bakers' two-room limestone Sunday house, there wasn't much to do except leave his bedroll and a few possibles there. Then he had learned that the stage wasn't due until two, an hour off. Over at the Nimitz Hotel, they brewed some damn good beer in vats in the cellar. The dark and hearty brew went well with lunch: sausage and sauerkraut.

Despite the good meal, something still wasn't sitting comfortable with Fargo after he saw how worried the station agent looked. The Trailsman didn't like the feeling in the pit of his stomach as he stretched his long legs and made another circuit of the stage station.

He decided to do something, instead of just standing around. The horse he'd rented for Kristina, a dapple-gray mare, stood at the hitch rail. So did his Ovaro, all saddled and just a few steps away. Fargo grabbed the reins and swung aboard. A ride down the rutted road wouldn't make her coach get here any faster. But it was a pleasant day, and a traveling man didn't get a chance to enjoy many of those in December.

There was just enough of a breeze to carry off the sweat as Fargo rode south, enjoying the sunshine and warmth. Birds scattered and chirped through the cedars. No, junipers, he corrected himself, marveling at how this short visit had already changed his speech. Another week, and he'd likely sport either a Texas drawl or a guttural German accent.

The road rose and fell with the rolling countryside. The trees grew thick hereabouts. They weren't big, not much taller than a man on horseback. But that was tall enough to keep Fargo from seeing much except when he was on a rise. Even then, his view consisted mostly of the taller hills, big rumples in a carpet of green.

Then things opened up, the influence of the Pedernales River. At its bank, a bluff at least a hundred feet high, the trees quit. The road veered to the right in order to get down the bluff, a wall of gray limestone, with horizontal layers and vertical fissures that made it look as though it had been laid by a master stonemason. Putting a road across its face must have been a chore.

Fargo paused and examined the route with a professional eye, to see if he'd have done things any differently than they had.

Several hundred yards to his right, the road got down to the river. But it didn't cross right away. Instead, it appeared to run downstream for a spell, close by the muddy, languid Pedernales. Maybe half a mile down the river, there was a broad spot, and above it rose a diagonal line that wasn't as weathered as the other limestone. That would have to be the ford.

With some of the road damn near in the riverbed, it wasn't any wonder why the stage company found floods so annoying. Fargo was within spitting distance of the ford when the stage, painted green like most Concord coaches and drawn by six mules, rolled up on the other side, maybe twenty yards away.

The jehu waved with his broad-brimmed hat, then halted and got down. While his mules drank, he went to the back wheels and knelt. His mild oaths carried across the river as he began to unhook the chain that held a log before the rear wheels. Chaining a log to the wheels was about the only way to keep a coach from going too fast down a steep grade.

That was when the first shot came out of the brush over on the coach's side of the river. Hit in the back, the stage driver tumbled forward, landing in front of the log.

The Trailsman didn't wait to see whether the man was still moving. He was too busy moving himself. There wasn't any cover worth mention on his sandy bank. He spurred the Ovaro toward the closest brush, a little ways upstream, and dismounted on the run, grabbing his Sharps as he rolled down.

Now the stage robbers were at work. Two appeared from where the shot had been fired, on the down-stream side. The one with a rifle sent a harmless high shot toward Fargo's perch, just to keep the Trailsman mindful.

Shooting back at them would mean shooting through the mules, so Fargo looked for a better opportunity as the coach door on his side sprang open.

The first man out was barrel-shaped and rather overdressed, considering. He sported a wide blue silk cravat that covered everything below his collar that his dark vest didn't cover. His round face, under a hatless head of close-cropped blond hair, was ruddy as he squinted upstream, toward Fargo, then turned back toward the gaping coach door.

"*Kommen Sie, fräulein,*" he ordered.

The two robbers were almost to the other side of the coach. Maybe it was their presence that persuaded another passenger to begin to step out. But more likely it was the twin-barreled dueling pistol in the broad man's hand.

24

He shouted something again, over to the two robbers, who replied and lowered their guns. The talk was in a language the Trailsman didn't understand, but that really didn't matter. Fargo knew enough. The stage was getting held up, and the rotund man, one of the passengers, was in on the crime.

The passenger he had just helped down—more like pulled out, actually—looked like a moving tepee with ruffles. She wasn't very big, but the green taffeta skirt spread so much that the stage company ought to have charged her for two seats. She just stood next to the door, mute, her face frozen and showing pale fear.

The fat man stepped back and said something to his companions, who were making sure nobody stepped out the door on their side.

The fat man was an easy target for the Sharps. Fargo exhaled slowly and squeezed the trigger, aiming for the thickest part of the man so that his bulk would keep the heavy bullet from pushing through and wandering off to where it wasn't needed.

The fat man spouted blood from the middle of his back and fell forward, his head landing at the woman's feet. He thrashed, spraying some red gore on the bright-green skirt, and tried to bring up his pistol.

Fargo cursed. Another inch or two higher, and that tub of lard would be dead now. As it was, he was gut-shot and wouldn't be long for this world, but he was still alive enough to hurt somebody if he managed to get that pistol up and aimed at the woman.

With one swift kick, she solved that potential problem. The pistol flew out of the man's hands. He rolled his head, saw that his hands were indeed empty, and went back to writhing in the sand. She looked all around, gazing longest toward the other passengers, who were beginning to stir inside the coach, and apparently decided that where she stood was as safe as any spot.

Where were the other two? Still over on the far side, where Fargo couldn't see them?

No, not now. They were scatting off through the brush, no doubt hurried along by the pistol shots that were now popping out of the windows on that side of the coach. The Trailsman sent a couple of sound shots that way with his Sharps. But that was mostly to hurry them even more. Those two were going to get away unless he tracked them down, and he was needed at the coach.

Everything seemed to be under control, so Fargo raced for the Ovaro. By the time he and the pinto were across the turbid Pedernales, the four passengers who had stayed inside were out. One young man knelt with the woman at the back of the coach, where they'd pulled out the bleeding driver. The other three, all middle-aged men of various sizes, seemed to be standing around the downed robber, apparently trying to make sure he didn't get up.

They stepped aside for the Trailsman, who got there just in time to see the robber take his last breath. The man's blood-spattered back swelled, then held. The air rattled out, and that was the end.

"Damn," the Trailsman muttered.

"Thought you were trying to kill the bastard," the tallest passenger observed.

"Some truth to that," Fargo conceded. "But once he couldn't bother anybody, I planned on asking him a question or two."

"You the law? A Ranger?"

The Trailsman shook his head. "No. Just happened along and did what any man should."

They all nodded, then the tall one spoke up again. "Who would you be?"

"Fargo. Skye Fargo." He paused, then looked to the rear, where the two were still kneeling next to the prone driver.

"What's the story on your jehu?"

"They said he might pull through, providing we stayed out of their way."

Fargo saw that they'd bandaged the driver, who looked gray-faced and trembly. The woman had a cup of water in front of him, and the young man, likely a doctor on account of the little black bag, was again checking the driver's pulse.

"Reckon they know what they're doing, so I'll stay

out of the way, too." He looked back down at the corpse. "Anybody know anything about this gent?"

"Sure didn't suspicion he was part of the robbers," the shortest passenger answered. "He seemed polite and all that, though."

"Rest of us got on in San Antonio yesterday morning. He got on this morning, just before we pulled out of Boerne, where we stayed the night." That information came from the passenger who hadn't spoken yet.

"Why were you running late today?" Fargo inquired.

The same man answered. "Some quicksand when we forded the Guadalupe. Not so deep we had to get out and push, but it still slowed us down considerably."

Fargo looked around the trio. The tallest was sandy-haired, clean-shaven, lanky, and not much more than a kid. The shortest barely reached his shoulder, and sported a dark, bushy beard of such extent that it would have served easily as a bib. The midsized passenger came in between; his hair was nondescript brown and he had a steer-horn mustache. They all looked a bit edgy, which was understandable.

The Trailsman pointed with his boot toe. "This gent talk at all? He have a name or anything? Any baggage?"

"Just a little leather case," the shortest volunteered. "Want me to get it?" Before Fargo's nod, he was climbing back inside to reach under a seat.

Middle-sized mustache broke in. "He talked mostly to the gal, though she wasn't much on talking to him. Had a fearsome Dutch accent."

"Dutch or German?" Fargo wondered aloud.

"German," the man corrected. "I keep forgettin' that the German word for German is *Deutsch*. So they say they're Deutschmen, it comes out Dutchmen to us, I reckon."

Fargo had already figured that much from how the robber had been hollering to his accomplices. "Search that gent's pockets," he told them, "while I look around."

First stop was the pistol the woman had kicked away, almost into the river. Although finely made, the gun wasn't really suited for armed robbery or much else besides a formal duel at twenty paces. Its twin

27

six-inch barrels sat side by side, each with its own trigger, hammer, and nipple. On the right side, both the barrel and lock plate were engraved with "C. Schilling in Mehlis."

So the gun was as German as its late owner. The dead outlaw couldn't have been on this side of the Atlantic for very long, or he'd have started using something more practical, like a Colt or Remington revolver.

Over on the other side of the carriage, there were boot prints. They looked a lot like those Fargo had seen by Tom Baker's cabin last night, but there wasn't any way to be certain they came from the same sets of boots. But for certain, the prints resulted from the same kind of boots.

Fargo gave up on squinting at the tracks when he heard some rustling that had to mean the woman was rising. He stepped over that way.

"Good afternoon, Miss Gottlieb," he greeted.

She looked more flustered now than she had before, when the robber had been pulling her out of the coach. "They said you are Skye Fargo, the Trailsman," she answered softly. "Good afternoon to you. Do you remember me?"

Fargo regarded her for a bit. Kristina wasn't much taller than she had been a few years back, when she was Greta's pesky kid sister. But she sure had filled out in the right places since then, and her hair, rolled back in a bun, still had that lustrous golden hue.

"Of course I remember," Fargo finally answered. "In fact, I was visiting your sister and her husband, and they asked if I'd ride down to Fredericksburg to escort you to their place."

She smiled and nodded. Then her face fell as she looked toward the driver, whose face still looked ashen as he took labored breaths. "That was so horrible," she added. Her voice was like her older sister's, but sounded much more American. Likely that was because Kristina had been so young when the family emigrated that she'd picked up English before she had enough German to give her an accent.

"How is he?" the Trailsman asked.

The dapper young man kneeling at the driver's side

answered. "If I can pull that bullet out of him soon, and he doesn't get infected, he'll likely live long enough to bore his grandkids with stories about this. But if it's all the same to you, I'd rather do the cutting under a roof."

"Sounds reasonable," Fargo agreed. "Is he up to riding in the stage yet? It isn't all that far from here into Fredericksburg."

The doctor nodded. "If we can lay him on a seat and hold him still, that ought to do for a spell."

Groaning and wheezing, the driver tried to sit up. The doctor gently pushed him back down. "Anybody have any whiskey?"

The short passenger stepped over with a bottle of Pennsylvania rye, which he'd found in the dead robber's valise. There wasn't much else in there besides a change of clothes and more bullets for the preposterous pistol.

The fat man's pockets, Fargo learned from the other two men, contained little of interest besides better than a dozen gold coins. About the size of American double-eagles, they bore the likeness of some distant and likely dead monarch. The inscriptions were in the same kind of ornate type sometimes used for the book names in Bibles, so Fargo reckoned the coins were German, too.

"Seeing as none of this gent's kinfolk have stepped up to claim his estate," Fargo announced, "I guess we'd be his lawful heirs."

The men laughed and divvied up the coins so that everybody, including the doctor and Kristina, ended up with three. They might not have been proper American money, but they were gold, and you could spend that anywhere. One leftover remained, which they said should be Fargo's reward. He passed it over to the doctor, who accepted it after a mild protest.

"Any of you men ever drive a stage?" the Trailsman asked.

No volunteers. It strained all five men to get the robber's heavy body into the rear boot. The passengers had argued some at the suggestion, but Fargo figured it was best to take the body on into town.

Maybe the sheriff, or somebody, there would have a notion as to who the fat man was.

Then the Trailsman made sure the driver was stretched comfortably on the front seat, with three men and the doctor facing him from the rear seat, where they were jammed together.

"Where am I to ride?" Kristina asked.

"Up with me," Fargo replied. "We need to talk some." He checked to make sure the brake was still set, then stepped back to finish the chore that had been started quite a while ago—unchaining the log. It wasn't hard, but a man couldn't help but feel nervous down there, considering what had happened the last time anybody'd tried to unhook the chain here.

Although most jehus looked nonchalant as they went about their work, perched up on the front of the coach, the job wasn't an easy one. Fargo knew what had to be done, but it had been a while. He was a bit rusty, but he'd manage, even if a ford, with a river right in front of them, wasn't the best place for a three-span team to start with a new driver.

After helping Kristina up, he gathered the six reins in his left hand and sorted which leather ribbons went to the leaders, swingers, and wheelers. He adjusted so they all carried the same small amount of slack, and noted how the broad-backed work mules responded by turning their heads.

Now for the whip in his right hand. Good drivers never touched their animals with the whip. The idea was just to pop it over their backs, which had a lot more effect than hollering or cussing at the mules.

He was a bit too careful with the first crack, since it popped about a foot higher than he wanted it to. But the mules still got the message, and the coach proceeded into the Pedernales.

Not until they'd climbed the far bank, with the Ovaro stepping along behind them, did he dare turn any attention to Kristina.

"Did that man say much to you during the trip?" Fargo inquired.

"Not much besides small talk," she replied. "He introduced himself as soon as he got aboard, and I responded, and then it was mostly the weather and talk of that nature. I had a front seat, looking backward right at him, so I could hardly ignore him. But he wasn't really forward or anything like that."

"What did he say his name was?"

Kristina paused. "I was afraid you'd ask that. His surname was Schmidt." She closed her pale blue eyes for several seconds, her face drawn in contemplation. "To the best of my memory, his first name was Johann. He only said it once. He was quite formal. We were *Herr* and *Fräulein* to each other when we talked."

Johann Schmidt. Same as John Smith. That was about as informative as being told the sun would come up tomorrow morning.

"He tell you his business or anything?" Fargo asked.

"He said he was going to Fredericksburg to visit his relatives for the holidays, just as I was."

"Did he tell you their names?"

She fluttered her eyes, then closed them for some more thought. "No, I don't think so. If he did, they didn't register."

She caught Fargo's scowl.

"I might have paid more mind to him, Skye, if I had known at the time that he was part of a gang that planned to rob our stage."

Fargo laughed as the coach caught some ruts, sliding them both back and forth across the seat. "Fair enough. It's just that you were there and I wasn't, and a lot of things aren't adding up here."

The middle-sized passenger stuck his head out. "Hey, Mr. Fargo, can you take it easy up there? Doc says this is hard on the jehu."

Fargo reined the mules back, but as soon as he relaxed, they acted frisky and in a hurry. Although it was hard to tell one part of this rolling forest from any other, the mules must have figured they were getting close to the end. They wanted to hurry home to grain, water, and a comfortable stall.

Having to deal with eager mules, instead of reluctant ones, was something of a novelty, but Fargo quickly persuaded them that he was in charge here.

"Skye, why did you say that things weren't adding

31

up here? Was there something different about this robbery? I've never seen one before." Kristina grabbed a railing, anticipating an oncoming rut that Fargo managed to veer around.

The swerve occasioned another shout from below. It also slid him against her, even though he had his legs braced. When he sidled back to a more respectable position, she sidled right along with him, her ruffled skirt pressed tight against Fargo's thigh.

Once the course looked reasonably smooth again and the smoke of Fredericksburg's chimneys began to waft through the air, Fargo answered. "From where I was watching, it looked like they were more interested in kidnapping you than they were in robbing the stage."

"Abduct me instead of rob the stage?"

"Generally, robbers get the driver down and then make him empty the boot for any strongboxes or the like. These gents started working when the driver was already down, and they just shot him. They sure didn't seem at all concerned about any precious cargo you might have aboard."

"Just mail and our bags, I think," she interjected.

Fargo continued. "And when Johann Schmidt, or whoever he was, got you outside, they seemed to lose all interest in getting the other passengers out so they could force them to empty their pockets and satchels. As near as I could tell, they just wanted you."

She pressed even tighter against him. "But Skye, why would anybody want to kidnap me?"

"Your folks are still pretty well-off, aren't they?" At her nod, he went on. "Maybe they figured on holding you for ransom."

"You mean you think they knew who I was?"

"Maybe not," Fargo conceded. "Could be they just wanted to cart off a pretty gal for their pleasure somewhere. You've doubtless inspired some young men in San Antonio to act foolish a time or two."

Kristina blushed. It took her a couple of tries before she could talk straight and change the subject. "Is that the stage station up ahead?"

"Just a farmhouse by the road," Fargo replied. "We're about a mile out."

Sorting everything out at the stage station took what daylight was left. They halted at the station only long enough to let Kristina and all the other passengers off, except for the doctor and the wounded jehu. Then Fargo took up the closest offer of a house for the doctor and his patient, and hauled them over in the coach.

Once the stage was done with its ambulance duties, Fargo returned to the station. As was customary for stage drivers, Fargo stayed atop, holding the reins until the tender got the mules' traces unhooked and led them back to the corral.

By then, they'd drawn more than the usual crowd, which included the sheriff. A tall man with a drooping salt-and-pepper mustache, Fred Wortman looked more competent than the usual run of small-town law as he asked questions about the holdup. But he, too, didn't have any ideas about Johann Schmidt. If the bulky dead man had been in Fredericksburg before, nobody there was going to admit having seen him.

"Guess I'm done with you, Fargo." Wortman laughed as they walked out of the empty stage station. "Glad you came along when you did. I want to thank you for acting like a Texan."

"Hope Texas doesn't have a monopoly on folks doing what ought to be done," Fargo acknowledged as he adjusted to the outdoor darkness, broken only by the lamplight escaping from shop windows and homes. "What's to become of the two that got away? A posse?"

Wortman shrugged. "Could try it. But likely it'd just be a waste of time, and most folks here have plenty of honest work to do without dropping everything for some wild-goose chase."

Fargo reluctantly saw the man's point. There was no chance of tracking the men until morning, and by that time they could be halfway to Austin or San Antonio. Nobody had gotten a real good look at them, and it wouldn't have made much difference anyway.

He and the sheriff shook hands once more. Fargo's next concern took care of itself. "Skye," came the call from the bench in front of the station.

Kristina rose as he turned to face her. "I was just

getting set to look for you and get you over to your kinfolks' Sunday house. Then I'll get a room downtown. I don't know this country well enough to be traveling it at night unless I have to, which I hope isn't the case now."

She stepped forward until she was almost standing on his boots, and then leaned his way. It seemed natural to put his arms around her, and foolish not to after she embraced his waist.

"Skye, after all this, and after what you said about kidnapping, I can't stay alone anywhere tonight."

He took a deep breath to take his mind off the way her breasts felt, pushing softly at his torso. "Well, then, I'll get you a room over at the Nimitz."

"No," she protested softly. "That's a respectable hotel."

"And you're not respectable?"

"Not if I check in with you. And I am not going anywhere by myself tonight."

Fargo wasn't of a mind to argue, which was just as well, because he doubted like hell that anything would change Kristina's mind right now.

3

Although the crackling logs in the stone fireplace provided a warm glow to complement the heat, the light wasn't of much use as the Trailsman worked at the myriad little hooks that ran down the back of Kristina's dress.

Undoing the tight bodice atop those billowing skirts seemed only reasonable after they'd settled on the low and overstuffed sofa in the Sunday house. In each other's arms, they were relaxing after a hard day.

Kristina, of course, was pretending that she had no idea what Fargo's hands might be doing behind her back. "Oh, Skye, I used to be so jealous of Greta. You'd come into town, and out she would go with this big, handsome, adventuresome man. I must have made a pest of myself."

Fargo chuckled as another hook came loose. "As I recall it, you were a bit of a tomboy then. You used to climb up in your folks' pecan tree and pelt us with nuts when you had a chance."

"Tomboy. I hate that word. That's what Greta always called me. Said that if I wasn't developed by the time I was fourteen, I'd never fill out, that I wasn't a natural woman at all. Just because she was all grown up by the time she was twelve . . ."

There. The last two hooks. Now the bodice was loose. And no damned corset beneath it, just a flimsy cotton chemise. "Well, it looks to me like you grew up just right, Kristina."

She shifted some, so that the Trailsman could start peeling the top of the monstrous dress down her arms. "I suppose you're an expert on that, Skye?"

"Been called worse," the Trailsman conceded. "But

I can't see any reason to think about any ladies I might remember when there's one so pretty right in front of me."

"You really think I turned out prettier than Greta?" She dropped her right arm from Fargo's shoulder, tracing her hand down his chest, to land in his lap. The massage she started through his trousers felt good, although it was aimed at a part of him that really didn't need any further inspiration. But it was a lot easier to start working that side of the bodice down and off when her arm was down.

"Kristina, I'll reckon that back then, when you pestered Greta with questions about her and menfolk, she told you to mind your own business."

She nodded. A few golden wisps, escaping from her tightly bunned hair, joined in the nodding. She traded hands down at Fargo's lap, so the other side of her body could escape from the bodice. "Is that what you're telling me now, Skye, to mind my own business?"

"More or less." He smiled. "What's important is what happens here and now. Nothing wrong with history, I figure, and memories can for certain be pleasant. But you've got to take each day as it comes, without fretting a lot about what might have been said or done before by folks that aren't here."

She leaned back abruptly, to Fargo's dismay. But alluring as Kristina was, he could see nothing but problems if she kept insisting on comparisons between herself and her older sister.

No, she wasn't fixing to get up and stomp off in a huff. She stayed put, and her sudden movement, aided by Fargo's hold on her loose clothing, resulted in her sitting there with nothing on above her waist except that flimsy chemise. Her firm, full breasts bobbed beneath it. The dancing light from the fireplace disclosed the erectness of her nipples, as well as the darker areolae that surrounded them.

"Oh, Sky," she sighed. "I'm sorry. I wish I knew better." She slipped forward to press her head against his shoulder. Now her hands were getting more ambitious, toying with the buttons on his fly.

"Better than what?"

36

"Better than to think about comparing myself to Greta all the time."

Fargo slipped the straps of her chemise off her shoulders, slowly, enjoying her smoothness and softness as his fingers played across her. Kristina apparently seemed determined to talk this out with somebody, and the Trailsman, whether he liked it or not, was going to be the somebody.

"Skye, all my life, my parents compared me to Greta. It wasn't just who developed into a woman fastest. If she played the piano, then I had to play the piano. Of course, no matter how hard I practiced, no matter how well the teacher said I was doing, it was just assumed that I'd never be as good as Greta." Her fingers were now playing an étude, maybe a concerto, on his throbbing shaft.

"And at first, she was so much the proper young lady and I was the skinny little tomboy who'd never find a husband. Then, when she started running a little wild, going down to the fiestas in the other end of town, and with gun-toting men like you showing up on our doorstep, my folks started worrying about me."

"About you?"

"Well, the way they saw it, if perfect Greta was turning out to be so wild, then it was certain that imperfect little Kristina would end up even worse. They kept wondering whether they should send me to a convent school so I wouldn't end up as a crib girl in some dive along the river."

Fargo moved a hand down and around. His progress was slow, because he was enjoying every bit of her he felt, but eventually he was rewarded with the satisfying sensation of a well-formed breast beneath his palm. His other hand slid down beneath the chemise, toward the small of her undulating back.

"It must have been a surprise, then, when she married Tom Baker and settled down," Fargo murmured as he massaged her in two interesting places.

"Oh, at first they were horrified that she married a gun-toting American roughrider instead of another German. They were sure that, if I ever did get grown up enough to be worth marrying, I'd end up married to somebody that was even more of a ruffian. And then, when it turned out that Tom was a hardworking man who wanted to settle down and raise a family, they all acted like I'd never find a husband half so good as Tom, if I ever found one at all."

She still gripped Fargo's stiff manhood with one hand. Her other had undone most of his shirt. Now her pliant fingers were sliding leisurely across his chest.

"Does sound like you couldn't win, no matter what you did," Fargo muttered. He hated the direction this conversation was going. His dislike was even more intense for what he knew he was going to do next.

The Trailsman's hands flew off Kristina. Getting up from a low couch was always a chore, and even more of one now, but he snapped himself to his feet, stepping back from the sofa, where a disheveled young woman looked up in astonishment.

"Skye, what happened?"

He fastened two buttons on his shirt before answering. "Kristina, I'm a man. I'm not a prize in some rivalry between sisters."

She pulled up her chemise, covering the luscious breast that had been so pleasantly exposed. "What's that supposed to mean?"

"It means that if we can enjoy each other for an evening, that's all it should mean. Maybe Greta was mean as sin to you."

"Maybe?" Kristina spat.

"Okay, say she was. What I'm getting at is that if you want to get even with her for whatever happened when you were a kid, you'd better find some other way. I'm not going to be the pawn in some game you're playing against her now." Fargo tucked in his flannel shirt, rebuttoned his denim trousers, and hitched them up.

Kristina showed no similar hurry to get dressed. Instead, she buried her face in her hands and started sobbing. "Is that really what you think I'm doing?" she asked her palms, choking out the words.

"From where I stand, it looks that way," Fargo replied, instantly wishing he could take the words back as her racking sobs turned into minor convulsions.

What the hell was he going to do? If he sat back down beside her and tried to resume where they'd left off, he'd either get a deserved slap, or else she'd continue to be willing, and he'd end up in some game he didn't want to be in. Greta, no matter how mean she might have been to her sister way back when, was still a friend. You can't do that to friends, and maintain much respect for yourself.

The sensible course would be to get out of here, go get a room somewhere. But he couldn't really leave her alone. Not with her in this condition. Especially not when there might be kidnappers after her. He turned and went over to tend the fire and add three logs.

Kristina lifted her face upon his return. "Skye, I'm so sorry," she whispered.

"So am I," he replied. "Sorry that you've still got problems with Greta, and sorry that things didn't work out different between us." The Trailsman paused and shrugged. "Sometimes I get too much of a bottle in me, and then I get to feeling awful sorry for myself, growing up pretty much an orphan after my family was killed. No parents, or brothers or sisters or nieces or nephews."

She caught his drift and smiled. "And sometimes you think it's a blessing to be so unattached, on account of the complications that can come from kinfolk?"

"You could say that," he agreed. "It's a caution how much people in the same house can hurt one another, even when they don't mean to."

She reached up with her right hand, pulling out what had to be the keystone of hairpins, because a cascade of blond curls fell to her shoulders. She lifted her left hand to smooth the golden tendrils back from her tear-tracked face, and the chemise fell, along with Fargo's eyes.

"You're telling me that Greta didn't mean to be so hard on me?" Kristina wondered.

"I've got serious doubts," Fargo granted. "Greta's not a mean-spirited woman, Kristina. She's like the rest of us. We do what we do, what seems natural at the time." He paused, savoring the sight of her ripe bosom while he searched for the right words. "And sometimes we have to pay for it later," he continued, a soft rueful tone creeping into his voice. "But don't set yourself up as Greta's paymaster, Kristina. There's a big world out there, full of other things to do with your life."

His tone got harsher, more commanding. "Even if I can't talk you out of wasting your time trying to repay Greta for those awful things she said to you, I can make damn sure you don't use me for currency when you try to pay her back."

Kristina settled back into the overstuffed couch and seemed to be gathering her thoughts. Then she gathered her skirts and stood up to face him, her arms reaching for his shoulders.

"Just hold me, Skye, won't you?"

He embraced her bare torso, pulling her closer to him as her capacious skirts pressed against his legs. She felt rigid and clammy as her face pressed against his shoulder and her tears moistened his shirt.

Finally her body relaxed and she lifted her head to gaze up at him. "Skye, you said that people want to do what seems natural, right?"

Knowing that he'd said too much, he stifled an answer and just nodded.

"Isn't it natural to want to be comfortable? And isn't it awful hot in here?"

Given the twin distractions that she had pressed against his chest, and the intensity of their conversation, Fargo hadn't really noticed how stifling the room was starting to feel. He must have thrown a log or two too many into the fireplace. Again, he remained wordless and just nodded.

"I'm baking under these skirts and petticoats," she announced, wriggling back a bit. "Help me get them off, won't you?"

Most of Fargo was glad to oblige, although something still nagged at him, even when she was pressed against him again, wearing nothing but a pair of lacy drawers. Finally, he spoke. "What's on your mind now, Kristina?"

"You and I," she murmured, her writhing body confirming her words. "You and I, Skye."

As her hands began to undo Fargo's most recent effort at getting dressed, they slowly waltzed the few steps back to the couch. Fargo's shirt was on the floor and his trousers weren't much above half-mast by the time they sat down.

Moments later, his fingers, probing beneath her only remaining garment, were exploring the quivering and moist flesh at the top of her thighs. Meanwhile his tongue traced delicate circular patterns, each delectable nipple getting its fair turn.

Somehow, Kristina found a way to remove his balbriggans while he slowly slid the soft material away from her waist, pausing to massage her rump and thighs. When his hands returned to her moist and open cleft, he knew she was ready.

The way she'd been exploring his tool with her fingers, she knew he'd been ready for quite a spell. Still, Kristina acted a bit flustered when he pressed her back against the couch.

"This couch is so narrow," she whispered, "and you are so big."

Her body knew just what to do, though, as one leg rose so that her knee was hooked atop the back of the couch. The other foot planted itself on the floor, and all the while, she was kissing Fargo so insistently that if he'd been in a worrying frame of mine, he'd have had to worry about losing his tongue.

With one limb pushing and the other pulling, she thrust up her hips to take him all in at once. The Trailsman advanced slowly into such delightful territory, enjoying every fraction of his deliberate progress.

"More," Kristina pleaded as he patiently answered her breathless requests.

Her panted appeals were replaced by a gasp, then a broad smile. "That's it, that's right." He continued to push. "There's more?" she wondered, spreading her thighs wider so that Fargo could answer the question.

Kristina found the floor with her lower foot so she could put more force into the frenzied way she began to rock her pelvis up and down. The Trailsman's hands slid down to her rear end, helping her out as well as giving more power to his own furious strokes.

"Skye, please, please . . . I want you."

He plunged to her dewy depths and exploded. With his first jetting spasms, both her legs flew up and she locked her heels together, forming a tight scissors grip that kept him in place while a relieving ecstasy swept across them both.

Not that he was in any danger of getting disconnected just then, but moments later, she had swayed her legs so much that they rolled right off the couch, down to the floor. Had Kristina been on the bottom when they landed, Fargo's size might have injured her.

As it was, he had to catch his breath before rolling across the smooth planks toward the hooked throw rug that had been in front of the couch before Kristina's enthusiastic foot had slid it away. Once they were on that pad of comfort, moving slowly and chuckling a bit in the process, Kristina released her grasp and sat back.

"This is kind of like riding a horse," she marveled, sliding herself up and down Fargo's shaft, which was responding with increasing vigor. Maybe it was the way she worked it with her internal muscles, or maybe it was the sight of her magnificent heaving breasts in the warm if waning light of the fire. Or maybe it was just because the Trailsman had been on a lonely trail for too long. He wasn't much concerned with the reasons for his continued interest in savoring Kristina, not as long as they could both be enjoying each other so much.

When morning came, as mornings must, Fargo was mildly surprised to find himself inside his bedroll. His first instinct was to nestle against Kristina and ask her just when they'd rolled over to get inside it. He didn't exactly recall doing such.

But she was still asleep, which stood to reason, since the sun couldn't be up yet. That was just the grayness of dawn, he decided after trying to look out the window. Some of the more prosperous folks had real glass, even in these part-time Sunday houses, but these windows were just oilcloth. You couldn't see through them, but they did admit enough light to let you know where the sun was. And the sun hadn't appeared yet this morning.

But all they had to do today was get over to Tom and Greta's place, no more than a three-hour ride even if you didn't hurry at it. So Fargo didn't mind a bit when Kristina, barely awake, wrapped herself around him and whispered something about starting the day right. It was fine by him, and he felt a lot more awake the next time he paid any mind to what might be on the other side of those make-do windows.

Still awfully dim out there. He grudgingly pulled on his balbriggans and gingerly opened the door, just a crack for a view.

The first look was so distressing that Fargo widened the door and stuck his head out. All that was out there was grayness, relieved only by its own swirling. No houses, no street, no trees.

Just fog. No, worse than that. Calling this "just fog" was like saying that the Pacific Ocean was just some water. He stuck his bare foot out into the opaque moist air.

His eyes had to follow his leg down to make sure that the vague shape at the end was indeed his own foot. Granted, he could see his hand in front of his face. But if he stretched his arm, his fingers vanished into the mist.

Fargo shook his head and pulled the door shut with a slam.

Kristina sat up. "Is something the matter, Skye?"

"Either my eyes went bad on me overnight, or we're in the middle of the thickest cloud I ever saw."

Kristina smiled. "Guess we won't be going anywhere today, right?"

"Would be difficult. I'm of half a mind to trail a rope behind me when I go to the privy, just to be sure I can find my way back."

"I've heard about these hill-country fogs. Tom and Greta say they're so thick that you can get lost on your own front porch." Kristina's arms rose and her face also beckoned the Trailsman, but he really did need to get out to the privy.

"Wouldn't doubt it a bit." He spotted the back door. "I'll be back in a minute if I don't get lost."

By crouching, Fargo could make out the path that led away from the flagstones that formed a back porch. He felt kind of foolish, walking hunched over like that, barefoot and dressed only in his balbriggans, but it was a certainty that no one would see him.

On his return trip, his feet were doing a pretty good job of sticking to the path. It was trodden down, unlike the rest of the yard. Every time his feet wandered away, there were cactus spines and loose sand to send him back to the straight and narrow.

But he shouldn't have been paying so much mind to his feet. He looked ahead, saw nothing but silver mist with swirling shadows, then looked down. Two steps later, something clubbed him in the forehead, rolling him back.

He landed on his rump. The Trailsman sat there for a bit, rubbing his forehead and wishing he'd had his morning coffee. Maybe that would help him think this out. What the hell had happened?

Fargo's eyes moved down to the path. It wasn't as wide as the one he thought he was on, and there were some acorns within the tiny circumference where he could see with any clarity.

The Trailsman inhaled deeply of the cool, moist air and got on all fours to follow this trail. Moments later, his suspicions were confirmed. This narrow path had been worn by little Billy, on his way to a live oak.

Fargo felt his way up its trunk, and this time he saw the limb that had jumped out of the void and whacked him. He felt mad enough at it to jerk it off the tree, but contented himself with grabbing a sprig of mistletoe.

Then it was time to get on all fours again and follow Billy's path back to the wider privy trail. He turned right and crawled along some more, and finally there were the flagstones of the porch. Fargo figured it was safe to stand up there.

Once he got inside, he could smell coffee brewing as

he raised his arms and stretched for some relief after getting around on hands and knees.

Kristina, clad in a robe she must have had in her bags, turned and rushed over to him. She leapt up to her tiptoes and planted a big kiss on his lips.

"What's the occasion?" he asked.

"Don't know as I need an excuse, Skye." She giggled. "But it is traditional."

"Traditional to kiss a gent after he returns from the privy? Or is it because he managed to get lost only once out in that godawful fog? Whatever it is, it's a new one on me."

She laughed deeply. "Well, I am glad you're here, Skye. Glad enough to kiss you and a whole lot more. But don't you know what you were holding over your head?"

He looked down at the sprig in his hand, its bright green leaves contrasting with the pale berries that looked like little pearls. "It's just a piece of mistletoe from a tree limb that came up out of nowhere and clubbed me," he muttered.

"Skye, around here anyway, it's a Christmas custom that you kiss people if they're standing under mistletoe."

He waved it over her head. With his other arm, he swept her to him and indulged in the tradition until the coffeepot started boiling over, with steam sizzling up from the stove lids. There was already more than enough fog outdoors, so the Trailsman released Kristina to tend to the coffee.

Fargo felt a lot better by the third cup. But there still wasn't much light seeping through the windows, and when he looked outside again, the visible world still consisted entirely of swirling nothingness.

"Don't these ever burn off once the sun gets high?" he asked. "Never saw anything like this."

Kristina shrugged. "I don't really know. Down in San Antonio, it gets foggy sometimes. But never this bad. All I know about these is what I've heard."

"And what have you heard?"

"That it just stays out there, thick as soup, until it gets good and ready to move on. Until it lifts, Tom said the only thing anybody can do is stay put. He got caught in one once on his way to town, and he tried to keep moving. He ended up over by San Marcos when he finally got his bearings. Said he'd never travel again in one of these fogs."

Tom Baker's trail-finding skills had never been on a level with Skye Fargo's. But Baker wasn't a man that got lost easily, either, and this was his home territory. Fargo realized that finding their farmstead today would be more a matter of luck than skill.

"Unless this fog lifts before noon, then, it looks like the sensible thing to do is stay put," the Trailsman announced.

"I'm all for that," Kristina agreed. "But all that's in the pantry here is coffee and salt."

Fargo nodded. "Maybe I could feel my way around town enough to find a grocer's. And it would be proper, I suppose, to find some Christmas presents for Tom and Greta and little Billy, since I've got a chance to go shopping here."

"You're sure you won't get lost out there? From what you said, you had plenty of adventures just getting to the privy and back."

Fargo smiled and tried to convince himself that he was as confident as his words. "As long as you're here, Kristina, I'll find my way back."

She fluttered her eyes. "You'd better. I've got some big plans for us for this afternoon, since we're stuck here anyway."

4

The Trailsman pulled his jacket tighter, but if that made him any warmer, it wasn't enough to matter. The cold drizzle still managed to work its way in, no matter what he did to his hat, jacket, and gloves. Propelled by a considerable breeze out of the north, the chill didn't seem likely to stop until it was resting inside his bones.

Yesterday's fog had lifted. Now the bottom of the dripping cloud was maybe five hundred feet overhead. So visibility was improved, although anything more than a few steps away didn't show as much more than a vague and shifting outline.

Kristina rode beside him, close enough for him to hear the chattering of her teeth. She, no doubt, could hear his frequent sniffles.

"This is one time I wished I had ridden sidesaddle instead of clothespin-style, the way you men do," she confessed to Fargo.

"Why's that?" he wondered, eyeing her buffalo robe with a bit of envy. At the livery stable this morning, she had insisted on a regular man's saddle, rather than a ladies' sidesaddle, for her rented mount. Fargo had just chalked that off to a family trait. The Gottlieb girls seemed to enjoy flouting conventions every now and again.

"Sidesaddle, I could keep my nether limbs together under the robe, so they'd stay warm," she explained. "This way, the robe flaps so much that it hardly protects me."

With a grimace, Fargo stilled his own chattering teeth before replying. "Guess I didn't think I'd need all that much protection from the elements when I finally came south for the winter."

Kristina laughed, shaking droplets of water off the drab woolen scarf she had wrapped around her round face. "Skye, you must have heard about the northers we have in Texas every now and again."

"Heard of them?" Fargo grunted. "I've been caught in a few that came so fast and so hard that they froze the songbirds right out of the trees. Some cold air comes whistling down from Canada, and there's nothing up there on the Great Plains to stop it."

"One minute the sun is shining and it's warm outside," she interjected, "and the next minute . . ."

"It's like this," he finished for her. "Dismal. Miserable." Another shiver started somewhere by his right knee and worked its way up. "Sure hope Greta's got her stove fired up plenty. Can't be all that far now."

The Ovaro's nostrils flared and the big pinto's ears twitched. Fargo looked down, wondering if they were on a slick spot, some ice perhaps, that would account for the horse's irritation. But his footing looked solid. Maybe it was only the way the wind had just shifted.

Kristina sniffed before smiling. "I can already smell the smoke from the chimney."

Fargo persuaded his gloved right hand to fetch a bandanna out of his jacket pocket. He blew his nose, then inhaled deeply. Shit. This wasn't just chimney smoke. The slight odor was acrid. The smoldering stench of burning cloth and foodstuffs ruined the pungent but pleasant aroma of burning juniper.

Before he could say anything, Kristina read his face. "What's wrong, Skye?"

"Plenty," he replied. "Prod that nag of your." He urged the Ovaro into a trot as they started up a rise.

Just under the crest of the following rise, Fargo reined up. The closer they got to the Bakers' homestead, the stronger the stench had grown. Now the reek was almost sickening. Fargo gritted and swallowed hard as he dismounted, Colt in hand.

"Stay put, Kristina," he warned. "You don't want to see what's over there."

She looked a little green around the gills, but wasn't about to give up. "If you can tolerate it, so can I."

"Stay put anyway," he ordered as he moved toward the crest, dreading the view he would get there. "I've got no time for jawing about this."

Remaining in his crouch, instantly ready to fire his revolver and duck for cover, the Trailsman edged forward. He wanted to sprint toward his friend's home, just on the remote chance that he might get there in time to do some good. But he wouldn't be able to do anybody any good if he presented himself as a clear target for whoever had caused the trouble that led to this disgusting stench.

So it was slow going, with occasional grim glances back at Kristina. The woman stayed in place, standing wide-eyed beside her gray mare, holding its reins as she pulled her robe tight around her.

Shit. The Trailsman fought off the green taste that crawled up and lodged in his mouth.

Thomas Jefferson Baker's dogtrot cabin now consisted of two heaps of smoldering embers. Only the smokeless stone chimney remained standing. Fargo made out the hunk that had to be the cast-iron stove, and moved his eyes to the barn.

That, too, had been fired, but it had fared better. Its roof gaped and its log walls were charred, but the barn still stood. The corrals and pens still stood, too, although the stock had been driven off. A goat had been butchered in the yard, close by the house; its skin and offal joined the clutter and rubble by the ruins.

Fargo sat on his haunches, fighting to remain perfectly still. Time to listen. Open your ears until you could hear the sizzle when a droplet fell and hit something hot where the fire remained.

No sounds of life, except for behind him, where the horses slowly inhaled and exhaled while Kristina's teeth chattered.

The Trailsman rose and wanted to turn around, jump aboard the Ovaro, and ride north. But instead he walked slowly down the hillside, every sense alert.

Tracks. Not all that distinct, on account of the small

rocks that poked through the thin soil, as well as the way that drizzle tended to erode the outlines. He knelt and felt the green stuff again in his mouth. Moccasin prints. Which pretty well meant Comanche.

Best, then, to hope that everyone who'd been home had been killed rather than taken captive. If there was a method of slow, agonizing torture that the Comanche hadn't used yet, that was only because they hadn't discovered it.

A few paces off, over by the goat's hide, the Trailsman found that one dismal hope had come true. He turned and succumbed to nature, retching up breakfast, before stepping in for a closer look.

Six-year-old William Barret Travis Baker would never get a day older. He lay there, grinning up at the Trailsman. Wooden stakes, chunks of barrel stave, had been driven through the boy's throat and belly.

The wounds showed hardly any blood, so there was some consolation. The boy had already been dead, killed by a tremendous blow to the head. The back of his skull had been smashed open.

Fargo's eyes followed the almost imperceptible sign to the chopping block, which squatted several steps away. The drizzle had washed most of the boy's blood away. But thatches of his hair remained, caught in the old stump's fissures.

A Comanche, then, had grabbed the boy by the feet and swung him in an overhead arc to smash out his brains. Then the boy had been tossed over here for further revelry. Fargo slowly closed the corpse's eyes and pulled the goat hide over the small body.

When did this happen? The hide still flexed and the boy's body, although cold, had not become rigid and stiff. The Trailsman gazed upward, trying to get some idea where the sun was in the sky, since judging by shadows was hopeless. He started estimating. They hadn't been in any hurry about leaving Fredericksburg, since they didn't have far to go, and there was always the hope, even if it hadn't happened that way, that the weather might improve if given time. So it had to be early afternoon now. Everything added up if this had been a dawn raid.

That settled in his mind, the Trailsman rose and looked back the way he had come. Damn, he wished he could see Kristina, but he didn't want her to see this. Best to hurry, then.

He scanned the yard, then circled the cabin ruins. Midway, the wafting smoke smelled so awful that he pulled a clean bandanna out of his pants pocket and tied it around his nose. Such tracks as remained visible were fading in the drizzle, and he didn't see anything worth noting.

Once away from the house, Fargo pulled off the bandanna. Just in case a stranger should ride in, he didn't want to be sporting a mask, which could surely give the rider the wrong notion as to who was responsible for this raid.

His strides long and rapid, the Trailsman arrived at the barn. Another body lay about a dozen feet inside the open door.

Even though he might have detected some motion there, he halted and drew his Colt. Then he stepped slowly to the wall and sidled, back to the wall, until he reached the door. His Colt went in first.

If it attracted anyone's attention, he sure didn't notice. Moments later, he was inside and at the body's side.

It had been Tom Baker, and his chest was still moving slowly up and down. So it might still be Tom Baker.

Fargo thought that for only a brief hopeful moment. Then he got a better look.

Baker's eye sockets held bloody pulp. His eyes had been gouged out, likely with a burning stick. Sometime before that, his eyelids had been cut off.

The man's mouth had been clubbed and hammered to where few teeth remained in place. It gaped open hideously, disclosing that the Comanche had cut out his tongue.

Farther down, his arms showed evidence of Comanche custom. They had been scraped in places, scraped deep enough to draw blood. The inch-wide wounds had then been rubbed with gunpowder, which stung like a thousand angry bees. Then the powder had been ignited.

Fargo didn't want to look any lower, but did anyway. Baker's trousers were around his knees. So were his blood-covered cods. He'd been castrated.

The Trailsman slowly patted his friend on the head, then brought his Colt around, placing its muzzle against Tom's ear. It was the only thing to do for his friend. He twisted, pulled the trigger, and rose.

Greta? Where was Greta? Ignoring what lay at his feet, he searched the barn with his lake-blue eyes. A few mounds of hay here and there, and three stalls. He kicked through the hay piles and lunged into the stalls. Nothing. The tack room was a clutter, as was the tool room. But no Greta.

Up the ladder in the loft was just half-burnt hay, some of it still smoldering, its smoke rising through the holes in the roof. The barn had obviously been fired from above, either with a tossed torch or fire arrows. No time to worry about that now. Where was Greta?

A shrill wail from the yard invaded the Trailsman's thoughts. He raced to the ladder and hauled himself down, reminding himself to be discreet about how he came out of the barn. The shot, his last service for a friend, must have attracted some attention. Comanche always ran as soon as they hit, though. Who could this be?

Kristina stood at her nephew's body. Her wail erupted again, a shriek that seemed to rise low in her torso and build up until it could no longer be contained, when it burst out of her. She stood straight, palms on her cheeks, as her mouth opened ever wider and the sound continued to grow.

She was catching her breath when Fargo got to her side.

"Kristina." She continued to stare straight ahead. He grabbed her shoulders and spun her to face him. "Kristina, dammit, hear me."

The woman's vacant and glazed eyes ignored his presence. She began to scream again.

Fargo couldn't really blame her for not staying put as ordered. She must have heard the shot and decided to look over the rise. And then she wouldn't have been able to keep herself from coming on down, no matter how terrible the sight before her.

He glanced around and saw the horses, standing nervously at the edge of the clearing.

Cursing the drizzle that was so hard on sign, Fargo pushed Kristina down slowly. "Don't move," he warned. "For God's sake just stay there." She began to choke and sob as she dropped her face into her upturned hands.

Fargo began a circuit of the farmyard, looking for tracks, broken twigs, dislodged rocks—anything that might tell him something.

Finally, over where he would have looked first if he'd been thinking a little straighter, where the trees came almost up to the barn and the barn blocked the view from the house, he found tracks. Any competent raider would have struck from here and the Comanche were experts.

The tracks led in and out. It was hard to tell now, but some of those depressions didn't look like moccasin tracks. There were narrow draw marks, like the heels of a woman's shoes might make. Short breaks and deeper spots suggested she'd been kicking.

In some disturbed junipers he found several blond strands. Beyond, in a small clear spot, just a few yards wide, were fresh horse piles. Many hooves had churned the soil that wasn't quite yet mud. Here Fargo spotted the wending, narrow game trail that the raiders had followed, in and out.

An unwilling Greta had gone up that trail just a few hours ago, after her son's brains had been dashed out and her husband's slow torture had begun. How much of it had they made her watch? How far had she been taken by now? What was in store for her?

Fargo didn't even want to start wondering about that, so it was almost a relief when he heard Kristina's wail again.

She hadn't stayed put, damn her. He found her in the barn, next to the mutilated body of her brother-in-law. All she could do was point and choke and sob before she finally grabbed the Trailsman for some support.

He waltzed her to the door before speaking. "Kristina?" he asked gently.

Her head rose from his chest. Her tear-rimmed and bloodshot eyes flickered. "No, no, no . . ."

"What's done is done," he answered, knowing it wasn't much consolation.

She interrupted when he mentioned that Greta had been carried off. "When?" she breathed.

"Early on today. Soon as there was light."

She collapsed against him, her body racked with shudders. He held her until she quieted. Finally she spoke again. "You mean that while we were . . ."

He nodded. By all that was reasonable, a tiny woman like Kristina should have exhausted her supply of tears about fifteen minutes ago, but she found it within her to resume sobbing.

He grasped her shoulders firmly and pushed her back, his hope rewarded as her stare met his. "Kristina, it isn't our fault. Don't make things any worse than they are."

"But if we had returned yesterday and you had been here this morning?"

"We didn't come yesterday," he told himself as much as her. "I damn near lost my way getting back from the privy. It took me almost four hours to run ten minutes' worth of errands in town, where I could feel my way from building to building. Going anywhere yesterday, let alone the dozen miles up the catch-as-can road to this place, would have been running a godawful risk of getting us lost in this damp."

"But if I hadn't come at all," she sobbed, "then you would have been here to do something, to protect them."

"And if I'd got into a good poker game back in Missouri, or somebody'd offered me some work when I passed through Murfreesburo, I wouldn't have been here in time, either. Don't blame yourself, Kristina. This isn't our doing."

It was about half a dozen Comanche raiders that swept through here, burning and butchering. That's whose doing this was.

But Comanche were a damn fact of life, like the

weather. It wasn't anybody's fault, really, if a soup-thick fog cloaked the countryside and made travel impossible, or if a northern swept down and turned a pleasant Texas winter day into just another icy winter day. Those were things that happened, and it was up to you to be ready.

Which was where Tom Baker had miscalculated, Fargo thought sadly. The man had started farming at least five miles from the nearest neighbor who might have helped him. And he'd been in where bands of warriors, as well as other folks up to no good, still wandered through.

But had Tom so much as kept a dog that might bark in time to give him some warning? And when he'd suspected that somebody was watching, had he even bothered to look? No.

Trying to change the subject that played through his mind, the Trailsman recalled that the tracks of the snoopers had been those of boots, not moccasins. Maybe there was no connection. But Greta had been hauled off, just two days after a gang of at least three men had tried to kidnap Kristina.

Damn little was making sense, and where was he going to start finding some answers? Tracking down Greta's captors seemed the best place to start. But could he take Kristina for what could be three hundred miles of hard riding? No more than he could leave her anywhere but in her parents' house, seventy miles and two days away in San Antonio. He sure as hell wouldn't feel right about putting her on the stage again. Right now, if he let her out of his sight and anything happened, he'd never forgive himself.

Some fog-laden rustling sounds wafted in from behind. Fargo spun, crouching as he drew his Colt.

The Ovaro was making the noise. For a moment, the Trailsman thought the horse was just looking for something better to munch on. Then he saw the hand grabbing the horn of his saddle. Below the horse's belly, a foot bobbed down into sight.

The Trailsman whistled, causing the Ovaro to begin turning toward him. Fargo hollered at Kristina to flatten herself, just in case there was another gun over there. He sprinted toward his right, hoping to get a better shot at the horse thief.

A mat of wet oak leaves slid beneath his boots. Fargo struggled to maintain his balance and his progress. He kept his feet underneath him, but for several seconds, as the Ovaro continued to move toward the woods, the Trailsman didn't get any closer.

By the time the Trailsman was moving again, the horse was almost into the trees. The thief was still hunkered on the far side. Fargo raced straight ahead, figuring that if he could get behind his horse before the growth got too thick, he'd have a shot.

Now the thief's slender back stuck out on the left side of the horse, bouncing considerable about thirty yards distant. There were some things a man couldn't take lightly. Fargo shot to kill.

In the slight interval that elapsed between the taking of aim and the arrival of the bullet, the Ovaro's gait jostled the thief, who slipped down. That saved a life as Fargo's slug plowed into one shoulder. Blood spouted from torn arteries, spreading down the baggy blue cotton shirt. The impact spun the thin thief forward against the saddle skirts. One hand began to slip from the cantle, although the other still held the saddle horn.

Annoyed by the commotion, the Ovaro swung back and forth. Unwilling to risk sending a bullet into his own horse, Fargo held fire and turned.

"Kristina!"

Slumped against the log wall of the barn, she looked up but said nothing.

"Kristina, come with me. Hurry, dammit."

For an agonizing moment, she remained motionless. Then she rose deliberately and began to step his way. She rocked her head and rubbed the tears from her eyes, which must have given her a clearer view of the Trailsman's commanding expression. Because she gathered her skirts and began to run toward him.

The Trailsman turned and whistled again. Maybe that would cause the Ovaro to slow down, or even better, stop in his tracks. Fargo trotted lightly along the horse's route. He arrived at where his bullet had met the thief; fresh blood now dotted the damp and twisting path through the oak and junipers.

Fresh blood wasn't one of the Ovaro's favorite things, either. So it wasn't much of a surprise that the horse was standing alone but looking perturbed on the far side of a clear spot, when Fargo came around a thicket, Kristina right behind him. The blood spatters went toward the pinto, but stopped at a small red pool, then trended off to some brush on the right.

The Trailsman halted at the thicket and held his arm out to signal Kristina to join him.

"What happened?" she panted.

"Some son of a bitch tried to ride off on my horse," Fargo muttered. "He's over there."

Kristina squinted through the drizzle, then nodded when she saw the outline of a man, low in the brush.

"Okay, you bastard," Fargo hollered. "Come out of there with your hands held up and friendly, and maybe I won't shoot you again."

"Shoot me," came the weak reply, not much more than a hoarse whisper with barely enough volume to be heard. "I ain't goin' back and you ain't takin' me back. Not alive, nohow."

Colt aimed at the form, Fargo stepped slowly toward it. "I'm going to decide what happens here. And what's going to happen is you're going to come out of there."

"Told you, mister, you can shoot me. But I ain't gonna be taken back."

The Trailsman approached within a few steps of the downed thief and paused for a better look. The form was clad in baggy blue denim trousers and a loose blue cotton work shirt. The wounded would-be rider was sprawled belly-down, clutching the ground. Vagrant twigs and leaves obscured everything above the slender shoulders.

This had to be a kid with considerable growing yet to do. Seeing one dead child in a day was seeing too many, the Trailsman decided. But he couldn't exactly ignore an attempt to steal his horse, either.

"If I have to come over and kick you, you'll come out," Fargo announced. "And I already feel poorly disposed toward you. I'd be more kindly if you'd just stand up and come over to see me."

The brush rustled as a head flitted. "All I can see here, mister, is the barrel of that pistol."

"Don't let it be the last thing you ever see."

The thief's skinny arms came back, hands sliding under the shoulders to bring up the torso. Although the stains remained fresh and crimson, the wounded shoulder had quit dripping blood. The waif who finally stood up straight should have been pale on account of the lost blood.

But it was hard to tell. For one thing, Fargo was blinking away a bit of momentary surprise. The thief standing in front of him wasn't a growing boy, but a grown woman. And her skin was black.

"Mister, just shoot me." With considerable effort, she stood straight, her dark eyes open wide and staring at Fargo's Colt. "Don't take me back just to collect the reward."

Fargo relaxed his grip on the Colt, but stepped back to have some distance—and reaction time—if this woman lunged at him. "Had a price on my head a time or two myself," the Trailsman said softly. "Who are you? What's your story?"

She gritted her teeth before answering in a brassy voice. "Minerva."

"Minerva?"

With some effort on account of her hurting shoulder, she shrugged. "It's the only name I got." She paused. "No story, mister, no story at all. Just runnin' away from Mr. Oakley's plantation. Tryin' to get to Mexico, like my man did."

The Trailsman motioned with his pistol, indicating it would be all right if Minerva sat down. He had a fair idea of the answer as he framed his next question. "Why did your man take off for Mexico?"

She glared at him for a moment. "Because they don't hold no slaves in Mexico, mister. If a body can get down there, she can be free. My man done it last year when Mr. Oakley was fixin' to sell him away. After that they got harsh to me, mister, mighty harsh.

Abused me fearsome 'cause they didn't have him around to punish. So I scatted off."

The Trailsman nodded. Reason enough to be skulking through the woods and grabbing the first horse that was within reach. "What's this about a reward?"

Standing at his side, Kristina answered. "When a slave escapes from a plantation, they generally post a reward. Two or three hundred dollars sometimes." She seemed to stop at something she didn't want to say.

He turned to her. "What else, Kristina?"

"Skye, there's a state law. If you happen across a fugitive slave, you're obligated to return her to her owner. If you don't, you could go to prison."

Various difficulties and complications started to play in the Trailsman's mind. Minerva interrupted the unpleasant thoughts. "So just shoot me if you was planning to take me back. I'd rather be dead than whipped again for havin' my man run off."

The Trailsman slowly holstered his Colt. "No," he finally said. "I've done a lot of things for money. But money or no money, law or no law, I won't take you back. Let's tend to that hole in your shoulder. Then we'll see what happens next."

5

"No, sir, I came upon that place while you and the lady were there," Minerva answered slowly as Kristina trimmed her bandage and the Trailsman asked questions. "Smelt the smoke and I headed that way, thinkin' maybe I could borrow a ham from the smokehouse or find a chicken that wasn't roostin' comfortable."

Fargo nodded. It seemed reasonable that this slip of a woman, while willing to filch anything from a ham to a horse, wasn't part of any general raid and plunder. "Okay, Minerva, let's start from the start here. No, not the start. I don't much care where in Arkansas I might find Mr. Oakley's plantation. And you can entertain us later with your tale of how you escaped. Just tell me what you saw and did yesterday and today."

The rail-thin woman sighed, then squared her shoulders. She sat up straight as she pulled forward from the log she'd been leaning against. "Mister, I couldn't see much at all yesterday. That fog is thick as gumbo. I tried to keep movin' on real quiet, but I guess I thrashed some in the brush. Them savages found me."

"Indians?"

She nodded.

"Where was that? How far away were you?"

She closed her brown eyes and mulled for a moment. "Maybe a mile or two from here. Not that far. Toward the north, maybe."

Fargo shifted the way he was squatting next to the woman. That didn't keep his thigh muscles from coiling up and smarting, so he stood and stretched before continuing. "The Comanche came in from the north and left that way. So that stands to reason. What happened when you met them?"

Minerva's eyes rolled. "I was already on my knees, mister, so it was easy to say some prayers. I prayed hard and plenty. Three, four of them came upon me. Looked me up and down."

"They say anything to you?" Some Comanche spoke English, so the question wasn't entirely a waste of time.

"Something about how they were looking for yellow-haired white men, not black white men. Then they just up and rode on."

"Black white men?" Kristina interjected.

"To most Indians," Fargo explained, "anybody that's not one of them is a 'whiteman,' no matter what color he is, or even if he's not a he. So they'd call Minerva a 'black whiteman.' "

"Mister, what are you fixing to do with me?" Minerva stood, flexing her arms and bandaged shoulder.

Kristina stood and smiled, justifiably proud of her handiwork. The bandage stayed neatly in place. It had been a tricky job, on account of how shy Minerva was about taking off her shirt in Fargo's presence.

Fargo shook his head. Another damned complication. "Minerva, you can light off on your own, keep going just the way you were going. Or you can come along, and we'll figure out something as we go along."

The fugitive pondered that for a minute. "I wasn't gettin' along all that good on my own, sir. But I surely do want to get to Mexico and find my man and get settled somewhere."

"I noticed." Fargo smiled. "I'll do what I can. I won't send you back or turn you over to any slave-hunters. But that's the most I can give my word on. If you believe you'll do better on your own, then do what you want."

Minerva's frown lifted into a broad smile. "I'll follow you, then, mister. Anything more you want to know?"

The runaway slave didn't have much more to say. After her encounter with the Comanche yesterday, she'd moved on, then curled up for the night in a pile of leaves. When morning came, she was hungry. That inspired her to move toward the smoke scent. There was Fargo's horse, which she'd tried to borrow. Anything to travel southwest and across the Rio Grande, more than two hundred miles distant, as soon as she could.

Which reminded the Trailsman that the Comanche were heading north, likely as fast as they could, with Greta as their captive.

He turned to Kristina, who was putting the bandages and other medicinal gear back into his saddlebag. "I'm fresh out of ideas," he confessed. "No matter how I look at this, we've got problems."

She buckled the straps before answering. "What do you mean, Skye?"

"If there's any hope of recovering your sister soon, I've got to ride fast and hard after those Comanche."

"I know that." She nodded.

"But I don't dare let you out of my sight, Kristina. Somebody tried to kidnap you. Somebody did kidnap your sister."

She paled. "You think there's a connection?"

Fargo shrugged. "I don't know what to think. Anybody that might be able to tell me is dead or gone. But the point is—"

"The point is," she interrupted softly but firmly, "that you don't think I should accompany you when you start after the Comanche. And you can't send me home on the stage after what happened. The only safe place for me might be my parents' home, and it's at least two days away. Which means a cold trail for you."

Fargo nodded slowly. "Greta could be in the mountains of New Mexico before I could even get started that way if I get you to some place safe first."

Kristina looked ready to cry some more. "Skye, I don't care how hard it will be." Her voice caught and she coughed a bit. "Whatever the sacrifice is, I'm willing to make it."

Fargo turned so he wouldn't have to watch her tears. The young woman felt guilty, somehow responsible for her sister's abduction by the Comanche. In a way, the harder the trip, the better she'd feel, because then she would be atoning for the mean way she had been talking about Greta—at the same time that Greta was being carried off after her family had been butchered.

It was time to scrounge whatever they could from the ruins of Tom and Greta's place, maybe some food and definitely some footwear for the barefoot Minerva.

When she started her escape from her role as a household servant, helping in the kitchen and doing a lot of mending between meals, she had been barefoot. That made it easier to be silent as she sneaked around the plantation that night, acquiring some foodstuffs as well as the clothing of a young man who worked in the fields. About the time she had changed clothes, the dogs started barking, so she never went back for her shoes.

Staying the night at the old Baker place made some sense, given that there was water and the like there, as well as a barn for shelter. But Kristina's anguished face told him that she wanted to leave as soon as they finished their dismal chores with the graves.

They moved up the creek for a mile or so before setting up camp. After supper, Minerva began to eye Kristina warily in the twilight.

"Ma'am," she finally said, her eyes lifting from the fourth finger of Kristina's left hand, which didn't have any rings. "Are you and your man married proper?"

Kristina blushed in the twilight and started to hem and haw. Fargo stepped in. "Minerva, best you mind your own business."

"But that ain't proper," she protested. "You two fixing to share a bed when you're not wedded. That's a sin in the eyes of the Lord."

"That so?" the Trailsman muttered.

"Mister, I can't read all that good, hardly none at all. They don't let us learn to read. But I do know for a fact what that preacher man said was in the Bible when he did my wedding. And then when my man took off, why that Mr. Oakley and his overseer, they tried to make me break the Lord's commandments and commit adultery, the way they tried to set me up with another man that wasn't my lawful husband." She glared at the Trailsman.

63

"So that's why you escaped? Because they were trying to make you lie down with a gent that wasn't your husband?"

She nodded. "That's a goodly part of it, mister. I won't abide by such. The Bible says it's wrong."

Fargo searched his memory. He didn't carry a Bible, but maybe he could recall something that would quiet this religious woman. Why hadn't he discovered this annoying fact before agreeing to allow her to accompany them? People always came up with new ways to provide unpleasant surprises.

"So you go by what's in the Bible?" he asked, and continued when she nodded. "Well, you running away from your lawful owner the way you did isn't what I'd call being real faithful to the holy scriptures. Doesn't the Bible say somewhere that slaves ought to be obedient to their masters? Did this Mr. Oakley tell you to run away, Minerva?"

Kristina, who'd been to church more recently, chimed in. "Judge not, lest ye be judged. That's what the Bible says, Minerva. And that ye that hath not sinned, let him cast the first stone."

"So I sinned when I ran away?" Minerva asked, her voice hushed.

"Does appear that way," Fargo agreed. "But we're willing to put up with your sins if you're willing to put up with ours." His eyes edged to Kristina, who was nodding in agreement before she turned and entered the tent.

Minerva's thin face was set and her short hair might have been bristling, although likely it was just the tight curls. She obviously wasn't ready to agree to Fargo's offer. Then a puzzled look flitted across her face.

"Mister, I hope you don't mind, but there's a question I've got to ask. Something I want to know. The lady here, Miss Kristina, she calls you Skye."

The Trailsman started to agree that it would be just fine if Minerva, too, wanted to simply call him Skye. But that wasn't it.

"My man, his name be Jupiter, he run off a couple times and got caught before he finally made good. The last time they caught him, the overseer told him that no matter how far he tried to run, they'd still fetch him back to Mr. Oakley's place."

"So?" the Trailsman wondered.

"Then the overseer said there was this white man that was part savage that could track better than any bloodhound. And they'd hire him to find my Jupiter."

Fargo agreed that he too had heard of professional slave-hunters.

"Well, this one that he be talkin' about, his name was Skye, like yours. Skye Farger or something like that. Not a name a body hears every day. And you was talkin' about trackin' them savages as hauled up Miss Kristina's sister. So you're a tracking man. Would that be you he was talking about?"

"Like as not," Fargo answered. "Skye Fargo is the name. Guess I never bothered to introduce myself, maybe on account of the curious way we met. And I do have a reputation in some places, though I've never been hired to track a runaway."

"Would you if you was?" she wondered.

Fargo shrugged. "Guess that'd depend on what the man was running from." His eyes moved to the blankets, barely visible in the darkness at Minerva's feet. "Now you make yourself comfortable somewhere for tonight."

She stooped to pick up the blankets and started toward the edge of their clearing.

"One more thing," the Trailsman cautioned. "Both those horses better be here, come morning, or you'll get your chance at finding out just how well I track and how mean I can get."

Minerva continued her slow steps for several paces before turning. "There's' some things a body just don't need to learn, Mr. Fargo. And anyways I do recall what the Good Book says about stealing other folks' goods."

"It's about time." The Trailsman chuckled. "Think on it some more," he added, then headed for the tent.

Considering all she had been through today—her nephew brutally murdered, her brother-in-law tortured in the ruins of the life he had tried to build, her sister abducted by Comanche—Kristina should have been the one who felt broody.

But it was the Trailsman who scowled and stayed silent as he slumped wearily against his wadded-up jacket.

"Skye, what's the matter?"

"I don't know," he grunted.

"Don't know what's the matter?"

He wanted to spit, but didn't. "No, I know damn well what's the matter. I don't even want to think about what's happening to Greta right now. And whatever it is is going to keep getting worse until I can catch up to them."

Kristina murmured something unintelligible.

"There's not a snowball's chance in hell that I'll catch up to them. Be hard enough anyway, with the lead they had before we got there. And with two women with me, riding double on a livery horse, they'll be long gone."

"But I want to go with you, Skye."

Although it was chilly, he wiped his brow. "What you want doesn't make much difference here, Kristina. It's what's going on out there that makes the difference. On my own, I might have a prayer. Now I've ended up with a fugitive slave. And I don't dare leave you by yourself."

"There has to be a way," she insisted, snuggling beside him and lifting his hand, pressing it against her breast, the nipple swelling into his palm through her thin flannel gown. "Don't leave me by myself, Skye. Not even tonight."

Suiting her actions to her words, she moved her free hand teasingly up his thigh before allowing it to pause. There she applied pleasing pressure that was impossible to ignore.

His own hands seemed to move of an internal volition, without conscious thought on his part. He found himself pulling her face to his. Their kiss was long and lingering. His hands, still moving on their own, found the hem of her gown and slid beneath it to savor the silken feel of her smooth thighs.

Kristina wriggled free of the kiss for a moment.

When she returned, the flannel gown was somewhere else. A luscious breast swept across the Trailsman's lips, which found a nipple in full bloom. A low-throated sigh emerged from deep within her as he nuzzled her, changing sides whenever she shifted position.

Meanwhile Kristina's small hands had been busy. The warmth of her touch meant that his fly was undone. The softness of her fingers indicated that his shirt was loose. The pressure of her palms, low on his back, meant that his pants would fall if he tried to stand up.

Not that he was of a mind to. He wasn't of a mind to do anything except enjoy what was before him. Nothing else mattered.

From her perch on his lap, Kristina embraced him again, then wrapped her legs about his torso. His throbbing shaft probed on its own, enjoying the textures, from satin to fleecy, that it found before settling against a moistness.

"Now, Skye, now," she breathed. She tugged at his body and rolled back. He went with her. Before her back had arrived at the bedroll, he had arrived in paradise in one tremendous stroke.

Kristina's gasp didn't have any suffering in it, though. She calmed for several seconds, then thrust up her hips in an effort to find out if there was any more. He gave her all he had. They developed a rhythm, slow and easy at first, of downward plunge and upward thrust.

The pace speeded. Down and up. In and out. That was all that mattered. The world was right before the Trailsman, enveloping him in soothing strokes. Pressure. More pressure. Pleasant pressure, but pressure all the same, that built and built.

Relief as they both arrived and began to shudder. He exploded within her. Her internal muscles tightened their grasp, to squeeze every drop from him. More. Still more. Total relief.

Still part of Kristina, the weary Trailsman rolled to his side. She nestled against him. "No, Skye, don't leave me by myself. Stay here," she whispered. "Stay with me."

They were still pretty much like that, all wrapped up in each other, come morning. Only one thing seemed sensible from that position, so the sun was almost up by the time the Trailsman emerged from the tent.

Where was Minerva? Not where she'd been sleeping, that was certain. Her blankets were folded neatly and placed with the other gear. But the Ovaro and the livery mare remained, so at least she hadn't run off with the horses.

After exploring silently for a couple of minutes, Fargo found her amid some trees, on her knees and praying. He turned softly away, figuring that wasn't any of his business.

His business was catching up to Greta. The more he'd thought about it last night, the more disgusted he felt.

Comanchero. It struck him as he reached to snap off a dead branch for firewood. The Comanchero might be the solution.

Most folks looked upon the Comanchero as a problem, which was fair. The Comanche did their raiding in Texas. West of Texas, across the barren Staked Plains, was New Mexico Territory, a good market for stolen horses and cattle. And people, too.

Like the Utes, their relatives and sometime allies, the Comanche often sold or traded the captives they took. A white woman might not make much of a Comanche wife, but sometimes the Indians could fetch a fair price for her from traders. For one thing, families would put up the money, a ransom.

And it was the Comanchero, a collection of people who didn't fit in anywhere else in the West, that ranged across the Staked Plains. They did most all the trading with the Comanche.

Fargo nodded. That might work. By making connections with the Comanchero, he might work out a trade for Greta. It would beat the hell out of riding into Comanche territory. And by now, that might be the only hope, anyway. Tracking anybody across the Staked Plains was an awful chore, even for the Trailsman.

The hopeful thought improved Fargo's disposition

all day. Besides that, yesterday's norther had gone on south to irritate people by the Gulf. By afternoon, the bright sun had dispelled all remaining moisture. Fargo relaxed and began to enjoy the mild day.

Although both he and Kristina had insisted that Minerva ride double with Kristina, the slender woman had refused. Nothing personal. Just that she insisted that she could do just as well on foot, unless they were being chased or something. Womenkind were contrary, Fargo told himself, no matter what color they were.

People on the run tended to be quite perceptive, alert to every nuance of their surroundings. Minerva was no exception. After Fargo explained what they were looking for, she did fine at finding and following Comanche sign.

The six mounted warriors had been pushing fast and hard. Such hoofprints as showed in the rock-studded soil were deep, at distances that indicated long strides.

The pursuit grew more complicated after they struck a wagon road that went north. The Comanche had used it, sure enough. The trick would be in discovering where they left it. Which meant scanning the edges constantly while the road rolled up and down through the trees.

So the Trailsman wasn't looking ahead as much as he should have been. Not that it made a lot of difference. He figured on following a trail, come what may, until something better offered itself. He'd have gone right ahead, even if he had spotted the three men on horseback earlier. But more warning might have simplified matters.

As it was, they rounded a bend as the road started to drop down toward a creek bottom. Standing in the road were three fair-looking horses, topped by three rough-looking riders.

Slumped in his saddle, the middle one sported a mustache. To the right sat a shorter, and much huskier, man with rheumy, bloodshot eyes, a brown beard, and a shotgun. The man on the other side had a beard that was even darker and more unruly. He was little, but toted some big hardware: a pair of long-barreled

Walker Colts in holsters that flanked, and hung from, his saddle horn.

Everybody stayed put for a moment. Then the middle one started talking, fairly loud and with an irritating twang in his drawl. "Howdy do?"

Fargo nodded and grunted a reply.

The man eyed the Trailsman, then Kristina, and finally, for what seemed to take hours, Minerva. His beady eyes returned to Fargo.

"Mister, I sure do hope you wasn't plannin' to be the one that turns in that wench for the reward."

Fargo looked at Minerva, who stood straight while glaring at the speaker, before answering. "Can't say as I was."

Shorty butted in. "Can't believe you'd just let folks ride up to you and take her off you after you captured her. Why, there's three hundred gold dollars awaitin' for him as brings in that there woman."

Minerva shrugged her narrow shoulders. While the three sets of eyes went that way, Fargo eased his hand down close by his Colt. When their attention returned to his lake-blue eyes, he answered. "I didn't say that, gents."

Mustache in the middle laughed derisively. "Now, you looks like a sensible man. Be hard for me to believe you was one of them abolitionists tryin' to steal her off. Stealin' slaves—that's a crime, mister."

Fargo nodded. "I've heard such. But supposing I tell you that she's all bought and paid for, and that I'd thank you kindly to let us be on our way."

Mustache laughed again. "Then I'd tell you that you was full of shit clean up to your ears." He turned toward Kristina and doffed his broad-brimmed low-crowned hat. " 'Scuse me, ma'am. Plumb forgot there was a lady present." He examined Minerva again and returned to Fargo. "If'n you indeed bought that wench, then you was buyin' stolen property, mister. For she fits perfect as the one that up and run away from the Oakley place, over to Arkansas, about three weeks ago."

The Trailsman shrugged, in the process moving his hand so that it rested lightly on the butt of his Colt.

"Do tell," he offered. "Meaning I'm out about seven hundred dollars?"

"You paid that much for a little one like that?" marveled Brown-beard, who hadn't spoken before. "Mister, if I had a handsome woman like yours, I sure wouldn't be spendin' that kind of cash for nothin' else."

Their eyes turned to Kristina. She'd been fidgeting, and now she clenched her teeth and shuddered a bit. Three pair of shifty eyes shifted her way as leers started to grow. Minerva looked toward the Trailsman and caught his faint nod.

The first man to take out was the quietest one, Brown-beard, who'd already been holding a shotgun in his hand. By the time the man realized he might need to use that scattergun, the Trailsman's Colt was aimed his way. An instant later, the .45-caliber slug slammed into the man's nose.

For a stunned moment, it looked like a third eye, even more bloodshot than the two that flanked it. The back of the man's skull exploded to give him a rose-tinged halo as tiny chunks of his flesh sprayed against his tall companion in the middle.

That man wasn't paying much mind to that, though. He had his hands full of saddle horn as he tried to stay aboard a horse that was working real hard at tossing off its burden.

When Fargo had started moving, so had Minerva. To his surprise, she hadn't scampered into the woods. Instead, she had jumped forward, bounding in between the other two horses. Her swift hands snatched the reins under the horses' necks while the men above tried to move their attention from Kristina to Fargo to their dying companion. Minerva jerked hard, jamming the bits up so hard that the horses were choking.

Understandably perturbed, the critters kicked their rear heels high in a vain effort to catch their breaths. Despite his hold on the saddle horn, Mustache tumbled forward. His lean nose slammed into his gray gelding's neck.

He snapped back up with blood pouring down over his mouth and tremendous pain showing in his eyes.

He loosed one hand, which cost him any chance of staying in the saddle for much longer. He swung his arm back round, flailing at Minerva. In case that didn't work, he was trying to get his foot out of the stirrup, so he could kick her.

Fargo's Colt barked. The slug caught Mustache in the chest, slamming him backward. Sprawled back at an impossible angle, he pumped blood out the hole in his heart. The crimson fountain smelled awful to the two horses, which got even more agitated. His dappled gelding tried again to bolt. That completed his last effort in life—getting his foot out of the stirrup. With his arm and leg free on Minerva's side, he slid off the other. He landed facedown in some dirt that started to turn maroon at the edges of his torso.

Shorty, too, had tried to get free of his mount, a small roan mare. His plan must have been to roll off the saddle, away from the feisty woman, and grab one of those long Walker Colts on his way down, while Minerva had her hands full with the reins.

Minerva caught the moving foot and dropped the reins of the other horse. Her left hand swung high and grabbed at Shorty's foot. Or more accurately, his boot, because Shorty wiggled free after a moment and his progress continued.

He was landing, on his feet and with pistol in hand, when Kristina's horse decided it had had enough of all this blood and noise. The livery mount reared back, Kristina pulled on the reins, and the horse decided to try lunging forward.

That slammed Shorty between two horses. It didn't quite crush him, because when the horses swayed out a bit, he had a little room to move. One hand, not the one with the gun, poked up from between the ribs. He was trying to grab Kristina, a saddle, anything. She didn't have anything in her hand except the fist she could make, which she pounded on his hat while hollering something shrill.

Fargo was of two minds. Dismounting seemed sensible, given how confusing things were getting. But then again, being on foot amid all these agitated horses was asking for trouble. And from a high vantage, he at least had some hope of figuring out who was where and what was going on. So he stayed put, his Colt ready, even though he sure didn't want to fire into that confusion.

While Shorty's hand was grabbing for her saddle horn, Kristina whirled her arm and punched his nose. Her horse started to sidestep, and it looked as though he might get some room to try using that monstrous Colt, which weighed at least five pounds. Why little men so often favored such big guns was a mystery, but Fargo didn't take time to ponder it.

Oblivious to the excellent chance that she'd get kicked in the head or chest by a flying hoof, Minerva ducked under Shorty's mount and grabbed at Shorty's thrashing legs. This time she got more than a boot as her hand clenched the man's slender calf and she dug in her nails.

That caught Shorty in midstride. He went down as Minerva tugged back. His horse, now rid of the choking pressure in its mouth, was now free to move. But the roan mare couldn't decide which way to go, since there was so much happening right beneath her.

She finally settled on going up. Minerva dropped Shorty's leg and sprang back, landing next to the longest corpse. Shuffling back, she stumbled against the body and rolled back, landing on her skinny rear end with her eyes still full of fight.

But the roan mare was even more angry. Maybe not. Could be that she didn't mean to come down with her lead hoof aimed right at Shorty's upturned face. That was likely the last thing he ever saw, because a moment later, he quit trying to crawfish away. He moved only when the mare tried to lift her front hoof out of what had been his mouth.

6

"Is something the matter, Miss Kristina?"

Minerva's piping question disturbed the Trailsman's morning reverie. He lifted his eyes from the lapping tongues of flame. With the arm-sized chunk of mesquite he had been holding, he fished the coffeepot out of the campfire and filled his tin cup. Without enthusiasm, he turned and rose from his crouch.

From the other sounds that had already disturbed him this morning, Fargo already knew what he would see. Kristina was weeping fearsome. She sobbed and shuddered as she stepped out of the low canvas tent to face the day. Minerva hadn't got an answer to her question, but that didn't stop her from traipsing over to offer whatever comfort she could.

The petite blond woman tried four or five times to catch her breath before it took. Even at that, her first efforts to speak didn't amount to much more than a couple swallowed syllables. Minerva grasped her shoulders and flexed them, as if she were pumping some air into Kristina.

"Do you know what day this is?" she finally blurted.

"Land sakes, I can't keep track of that, not out here," Minerva answered. "Back to Mr. Oakley's, we could just count from Sunday to Sunday, but how's a body to know Sunday from any other day in this wilderness?"

Fargo was thinking out loud. "Seems to me it'd be a Monday . . . No, that's not it! Went to Fredericksburg on Thursday—wasn't it?—so this'd be a Sunday . . ."

"Not that," Kristina protested, her round face growing even redder beneath her trailing tears. "Who cares if it is Sunday or Tuesday? Don't you know this is Christmas?"

That was enough for Minerva, who stepped back, holding her angular face in her long fingers. "Goodness' sakes, that's right," she agreed. "This would be Christmas Day."

Fargo shrugged. "Stands to reason, when I think of it." He paused, uncertain as to what to say next. "But what are we supposed to do? Want me to chop down a tree? Think we should lay over today instead of moving on? I doubt like hell that the Comanche take the day off."

Kristina turned to Minerva for some reinforcement before glaring his way and sputtering some. "Perhaps not," she sobbed. "But we cannot let Christmas pass as though it were just another day. It's a special day, a day for families to . . ."

"She be right, Mr. Fargo," Minerva agreed as Kristina got caught by her own choking sobs. "This is a holy day."

"Yes, you're right. We can't just let Christmas go by without doing something special," Fargo replied. "Do you have anything in mind?"

Minerva spoke up. "Christmas Day. Don't you white folks always give each other presents on Christmas Day?"

Kristina turned to her. "Don't you?"

Minerva chuckled. "We try, ma'am, we try. But we don't have much."

Fargo turned away and, with long, deliberate strides, walked over to his saddlebags.

In one he found a lumpy parcel, wrapped in rough brown paper, about the size of a small loaf of bread. Kristina had brought that up from San Antonio. He reached into the other and brought up a similar parcel, gifts he had purchased when feeling his way through the fog in Fredericksburg.

Slowly he walked back to the center of camp. Kristina began crying more, softer this time. "Here they are." That was all he could think of to say.

Now it was Minerva who was getting more distraught. "Mr. Fargo? Miss Kristina? I don't have nothin' to give you folks. And you've been so good to me, 'specially after you caught me tryin' to make off with your horse, and then when them slave-hunters come up to us, you, well, you surely did go to a lot of trouble on account of me." She tried to say more, but she had succumbed to melancholy.

The Trailsman interrupted her sobs. "Try giving us a smile. We sure as hell need one around here."

Minerva looked up, tears still trickling down her lean face. "It's powerful hard to smile when a body don't feel like smilin'."

"That's a fact," Fargo retorted. "But that's the time you need a smile most. Come on. Give it a try."

"You mean like this?" She pushed a broad grin across her thin and tear-streaked face.

"No, more like this." Fargo grabbed the tendrils of beard on each cheek and pulled his face out and up. He must have looked pretty stupid, because Kristina decided she could do better.

"That's not a smile, Skye." She puffed out her round cheeks. Moments later, her pursed lips rose. "This is a smile," she managed to sputter before an attack of giggles got her.

"Let's figure out these presents, then." The Trailsman laughed. "And remember, no frowning." He started to undo the wrapping paper on his parcel.

Kristina began to spout some real laughter from deep within.

"What's so funny now?" He got a hold of Billy's present.

"Have you ever heard of Santa Claus? He's part of our German celebration."

"Santa Fe, I've heard of. And Santa Anna, of course. But Santa Claus?" The Trailsman mulled for a moment. "Oh, sure. Guess I've got his job today, handing out presents."

"But he's short and fat and wears a red suit." Kristina giggled. "You're tall and lean and—"

"Best you settle for what you can get today," Fargo interjected. "And we've both got beards, don't we, even if mine's black and his is white?" He fished out Billy's present, a store-bought slingshot with a leather pouch and genuine gum-rubber pulls. The Trailsman struggled hard to keep his smile, which wasn't easy when he realized that the kid would never use it to break a window or plunk the rump of a passing horse.

"This won't be of much use to any of us. But this might be, so that you gals can improve your smiles." He pulled out the hand mirror he had purchased for Greta. "Not that your pretty faces aren't fetching enough at the moment, but a little practice never hurt anybody, now, did it?" He handed it to Kristina, who gazed at her own reflection for a moment before passing it along to Minerva.

The jug of good sipping whiskey, his present for Tom, came up next. "Ah, now here's something we can all use." The Trailsman considered draining it right here and now. Greta was likely getting farther away by the moment, if she wasn't being abused. If she wasn't dead by now. But you do what has to be done, and what had to be done now was celebrate Christmas.

His forced jocularity was taking every bit of effort he could muster. He struggled and managed to maintain his facade as he loosened the wrapping of Kristina's bundle.

"Apples?" he wondered aloud. "Enough here for each of us to have two."

He handed the biggest and reddest one to Minerva, who looked dubious. "Land sakes, Mr. Fargo, you know what troubles came long ago when the first woman bit into one of these."

"Well, I don't look much like Santa Claus, but I know I look even less like that old serpent," Fargo rejoined before taking a big chomp out of his. He passed one to Kristina.

She nibbled a bit. "For some reason, they don't grow apples in this part of Texas. My sister always said she missed them so. Do you know how hard I had to look around San Antonio before I found these?"

"Much appreciated," Fargo mumbled between bites. The mushy flesh of the fruit was a long way from being crisp and fresh, but this wasn't the time to mention that.

"Now, see here," he continued, "we're going to have some music with our dinner. Can't say we don't celebrate properly here." He pulled out two harmonicas, one about as long as his hand, and the other smaller, sized for a youngster.

"We can make our own melodies with these." He passed one to each woman. "Since music isn't among my many talents," he continued, his voice starting to sound like a carnival barker's, "I shall be forced to content myself with this." He opened the tiny music box that Kristina had purchased for her sister.

Atop his hefty palm, the delicate machinery inside began to whir, followed by a tinkling song. The rising tune sounded something like church music, which was likely why Fargo couldn't place it.

Kristina read the question in his eyes. "It's a song by Johann Sebastian Bach. 'Jesu, Joy of Man's Desiring.' It was one of Greta's—it's one of my favorite songs." Both she and Minerva were nodding along with the song.

Amid the agreeable music, other sounds, disquieting ones, reached the Trailsman's ears. Considerable rustling in the brush. Low limbs brushing one another and snapping off. Grunts and growls, maybe. Ground getting pounded on and poked at. A lot of rumble out there somewhere, kind of like a buffalo stampede, except not nearly so immense.

Keeping his smile as the music box played on, the Trailsman scanned the campsite. Nothing besides the usual clutter. His eyes moved across the clumps of grass, over the scattered acorns and pecans amid the sharp gravel, past the knee-high eruptions of long-spined cactus—cow's-tongue prickly pear that looked like a bunch of plates glued together at impossible angles.

The horses had their ears up and their nostrils open. They sensed something, although they didn't look all that agitated by it. Even as the low rumbling sound grew closer and louder, the mounts stayed put, as if they were waiting to see the show.

But what on earth was going to show? The music box lost its enchantment for the women as they looked up to meet the questioning gaze above his smile.

"Mr. Fargo, Miss Kristina, get up in a tree. Fast," Minerva said. "Waste no time. They come after me once." She scurried for a post oak and planted her foot in its low crotch, then grabbed a limb overhead and started pulling her lithe body up. Kristina's head snapped from the fugitive to Fargo. Then she gathered her skirts and followed Minerva.

Before the Trailsman could do much more than give Kristina a boost, the first invaders pounded into the campsite clearing.

Mostly dark, although they came in several colors, they looked much like regular farm pigs, except thinner. From a broadside view, there wasn't much difference. Head-on, the way most of the porkers charged toward the Trailsman, their massive heads were wider than their lean bodies. Razorback hogs. Their hams weren't much, although they produced tolerable bacon.

Unlike lazy farm pigs, these grunting hogs were quick and nimble. Their sharp, finger-size tusks glinted in the sun as they rushed toward Fargo, surly sows at their sides. They seemed to figure that if anybody was going to be dinner today, it would be the Trailsman, not them.

Fargo didn't agree, of course. His drawn Colt barked at the nearest one. No, the wounded pig, squealing loud and awful, wasn't the nearest one. Fargo discovered that when he turned and started toward the nearest tree that was big enough to hold his weight.

Right at his boots, a boar that outweighed him lowered its head and planted a tusk in the Trailsman's calf. Boot leather wasn't much protection against the force of several hundred pounds of pig. The bloody tusk came free when the hog pulled back, ready for another try.

Taking the wild pigs one at a time was about all the Trailsman could do. His Colt plugged the boar between its hairy, upthrust ears. But the smell of blood from his leg had attracted a hungry crowd in back. Without turning, he kicked blindly at them, to little effect.

It stood to reason that being kicked in the nose wouldn't bother them much. They used their big snouts all the time to root around in this rocky ground. Now one had its teeth in the Trailsman's right boot. He tried to wrest his foot forward so he could get both feet under him. Falling down in this crowd didn't look like a good idea.

His injured left leg stung. It was the target for another big boar. It lunged forward, jaws open. Fargo couldn't dodge the charge. His snapped shot, into the swine's massive and frothy jowls, would certainly kill the critter. But not for a couple of minutes, and until then, the angry, dying beast figured on making the Trailsman its last meal.

He was grateful for Minerva. She'd been skulking through these woods for the past fortnight, so she had known what was coming in time for the women to climb to safety. But there hadn't been a tree within reach that was stout enough for the Trailsman.

Fargo had seen, hunted, and eaten his share of javelinas and peccaries. But this was the first time he'd seen so many wild pigs in one place and so close. Everywhere he dared to look, except for up in the trees, there were milling hogs.

His Colt was useless, as useless as teats on a boar. He could kill one with every round, and there'd be ten to take each voracious victim's place. The throwing knife in his boot was out of reach. His belt knife had one advantage. You couldn't run out of ammunition for it. But while you were sticking one pig, another dozen would be coming at you.

The boar that had been trying to chew at his wounded leg hadn't done much more than rip his jeans to tatters when it finally rolled over and died from its head wound. And suddenly, the pressure eased on his boot, so he could swing the extended leg forward. He had both feet on the ground again as the pigs surged at him.

A heaving tusk grazed the knee of his good leg. Some teeth grabbed his boot. Fargo swung his Colt down. The powerful blow discouraged that porker, but two more shouldered their way in.

Fargo tried to keep himself from sagging. His only hope was to stay upright, but his legs couldn't take much more of this abuse. Sharp hooves pummeled his boots as more pigs jostled and stabbed at him.

The two boar's bodies slowed the charge some. But every step was agony, the way the pain surged up from his blood-spurting legs. And even if he'd had steel legs, there were so many pigs milling around, so closely packed, that he likely couldn't have taken many steps anyway.

Fargo clubbed and flailed with pistol and knife. He was more than a match for any dozen wild pigs, no matter how big and mean. Trouble was, there were at least a hundred in this herd. He did have moments of satisfaction when his pistol butt would catch one between its beady eyes and the brute crumpled, to become a minor impediment for its cohorts as they scrambled over the carcass to continue the assault.

With his slashing belt knife, he sometimes managed to lop off an ear. Their skulls were too thick for a knife to matter there, and stabbing their narrow backs just made them even madder. Twice he jabbed eyes. One casualty, too shocked to do much more than add its anguished squeal to the ear-shattering cacophony, stayed around long enough for the Trailsman to slit its throat.

For a moment, the herd seemed distracted. Something else caught its attention. Fargo took advantage of the lull to leap for the closest collection of downed pork. Four bodies, two still heaving, formed a square just big enough for him to crouch in.

First things first. He slit the throats of the two living swine. He lifted his head in time to face a charging boar at arm's length. Abruptly it changed course as an acorn thudded between its tiny eyes.

The sow charging from the rear ended up becoming part of the Trailsman's barricade. But it was touch and go for a second as she lunged for his neck. His knife got to hers first. So much raw red blood gushed that Fargo's eyes were covered.

Once he wiped his face, he noticed things had quieted down out there. The noise was still disgusting, with the agonized shrieks of the wounded. The way his legs and feet were hurting, Fargo felt a lot like joining them in their vocal anguish. But he gritted his teeth and felt better when he realized that most of the low grunting had vanished.

The Trailsman sat up straighter and looked out from behind his bloody, bristled barricade. Most of the pigs had gone, and the dozen or so that remained, and were able to move, were scampering on out of the clearing. A small one, not long from the litter, jumped with a start and began to trot toward the trees. The others joined it.

Trees. Fargo swung his head toward the oak that stood closest to where the women had been standing just before this all started. Straddling a limb, they both looked safe enough. Their feet hung pretty low, but still out of the reach of the hogs.

As he watched, Minerva spotted another laggard and loosed an acorn at it from the slingshot. Stung in the rump, the razorback sprang forward and departed the clearing with some urgency.

A few others still milled about, perhaps twenty feet from the Trailsman. He was about to get up and see if he could outrun them to a tree when they, too, lost interest in coming his way. When they lifted their heads toward him, a bright flash passed across their brows. Through the swirling haze of churned-up dust, Fargo traced the rays of light back to Kristina.

She was using that hand mirror to reflect the sun's blinding glare into the pigs' eyes. Whenever they started toward the Trailsman, they got a faceful of sunshine, which tempered their enthusiasm for charging him.

Within a minute, the clearing was free of any swine that were able to get out of it. Splattered with blood, his own and the animals', Fargo rose. Now all that disturbed the clearing were the shrill and piercing last squeals of several wounded hogs. He ended their agonies with his knife before hobbling over to the tree.

"Lord Almighty, Mr. Fargo. You didn't have to go to such trouble to fetch us a pork roast for Christmas dinner," Minerva announced.

Although his scraped and punctured calves and shins kept shooting surges of burning pain upward, Fargo found himself smiling. "Seemed only proper," he replied. He sagged a shoulder against the trunk. He needed all the help he could find if he was going to stand up here. "But one would have been more than enough, I figure. At least I wasn't all that hungry."

"Well, I count at least a dozen out there," Kristina

proclaimed. She handed the mirror down to him and began to sidle back along the limb, on her way down. Fargo lifted a hand, which she grasped before alighting. Minerva followed.

"Sure glad you thought of climbing these trees. Just wish there'd been a bigger one close by," he whispered hoarsely to Minerva. He didn't plan to whisper. It was just all the voice that he could muster between clenched teeth.

"That's what I did when I saw them comin' at me one morning," she said. "Shinnied right up a tree and watched 'em go by."

"Reckon I'll know better next time." The mirror was still in his hand, the hand between his trunk and the tree's. "I want to thank you for figuring out some way to distract those critters before they had me for Christmas dinner."

While they nodded and chattered something about how they'd used what they had at hand, he brought up the mirror. He couldn't help but stare at the blood-shrouded face that flashed before him.

His beard and shoulder-length hair were matted with congealed blood. In some struggle, a hoof had hammered one of his high cheekbones, scraping his face open and leaving a plum-colored bruise that was big and still getting bigger. When did that happen? He couldn't remember. Fights were like that. You never knew how much you got hurt until the heat had gone out of the battle. Then the pain would remind you of what happened.

The Trailsman passed the mirror on. His eyes dropped to his legs. Or what was left of them. From knees on down, there was just blood and flesh, a coating of sticky gore that sprouted a few clumps of bristle. That wasn't his, he knew, but of the rest, he couldn't tell what had come from him and what was a contribution from the hogs.

Except the hogs were out of their misery, and his was getting worse by the second. He felt light-headed and edged closer to the tree, shuddering.

"You sit down, Mr. Fargo, and let us tend to you," Minerva declared. "You'll die for certain of the blood poisoning if you don't clean those wounds."

The Trailsman got an arm around the trunk and steadied himself. "The horses. Our camp. Dinner. Got to gut and skin one of those hogs before the meat gets spoiled."

"Sit down, Skye," Kristina ordered. She spun, whirling her skirts. After staring outward for about a minute, the blond woman swirled back his way. "The horses look all right. We saw them kicking."

"Must have discouraged the hogs," Fargo grunted.

Kristina ignored him and went on. "The tent got pushed down. Our gear is scattered and the hogs must have trampled some of it. But I believe we can manage." She paused and glared at him. "If we can get you to sit down and let us tend to that leg."

Standing up was getting to be an awful lot of work anyway. Fargo released his embrace on the tree and turned, sliding his back down its surprisingly smooth bark until his rear end hit the ground. "Okay, I'm sitting. You gals happy now?"

Kristina glared back at him. "Skye, we must clean those wounds. It's easier when you're sitting down." She knelt beside his legs and started peeling off the tatters of his jeans. Her eyes lifted to meet Minerva's. The angular black woman scurried away, returning shortly with a canteen as well as bandages from his saddlebag.

Fargo tried to keep his mind on something else while they poured salt and red-hot needles into the open spots. At least that's what it felt like they were doing. It helped a lot that the jug of whiskey had landed in a soft spot, and had somehow emerged unbroken despite all those milling hooves.

The Trailsman tried to lift it for another swig. The jug should be getting lighter. Stood to reason, anyway. But instead, the damn thing kept getting heavier. He got a better grip on it. Still it wouldn't rise. Moments later, he was snoring.

7

The afternoon sun seemed intent on burning its way through the Trailsman's face, past his skull, to bake his brains when he awoke from his bourbon-inspired nap. He pulled his elbows back and perched on them to lift his torso.

Getting a look at things seemed like a good idea, but he waited to open his eyes. He hurt. Hurt like hell. Even with the sun out of his face, powerful surges of pain dominated his consciousness. It took several slow, deep breaths before he felt calm enough to study on it.

Hangover? No, he hadn't swilled all that much whiskey. Enough to feel comfortable after that run-in with those wild hogs, but not enough to make a man feel like this. Besides, hangovers pounded your head. His head was sure aware of this pain, which alternated between a potent but dull ache and intense sizzling spasms. But the pain was coming from somewhere else.

Comanche. That made sense. They'd captured him while he was foolishly napping, and now they had him staked out while a few old women tortured him for the amusement of the rest of the tribe. He told his head to quit hurting and to quit dreading, and to start listening. Nothing like the chatter of an Indian village.

His left leg. That's where most of that hurt was rising from. Look at it, then, after he'd looked around.

He was still under the oak where he'd fallen asleep. A few yards away, Kristina and Minerva went about tidying up camp. They had reassembled the gear—or most of it, anyway. Now they were wrestling with the tent. Every time they got one guy rope taut and pegged, another would slacken. The little canvas tent sagged, and they'd try again.

The two women didn't seem concerned by anything else, though. The horses, about thirty yards off, didn't look troubled, either, as they stood about, placidly munching on such grass as they found.

So Fargo figured he didn't have to worry about much besides that throbbing left leg, either. He looked down at his own body and started to laugh. He couldn't help it. In cleansing his wounds, the women had snipped off the legs of his trousers, just above the knees. But he still had his boots on. It looked like they had pulled off his boots and cleaned them off, washed all the blood and gore off his feet, and then reshod him, complete with clean socks.

Trying to ignore how foolish he looked to himself without a full set of pants, he examined his bare legs. A few puncture wounds had been neatly bandaged. Some scrapes had been cleaned but not covered. Just off the shin of his left leg, a long gash had also been left open. It wasn't bleeding, but it wasn't closed all that well, either. The damn hole would likely need to be sewn shut before he'd be able to move the leg without filling his boot with blood.

His stirring attracted attention. Minerva noticed first and said something to Kristina, who led them his way. "Skye, you're awake."

He nodded, surprised by how groggy he still felt.

"Goodness' sakes, Mr. Fargo, those pigs did quite a job on you," Minerva added, looking at his legs.

Again he nodded. "Does look that way." All three sets of eyes met at the long gash.

Kristina broke the silence. "That wound will not heal unless the sides are stitched together." Her eyes met his question. "We found a suitable needle in your gear, but the only thread you have is cotton. We didn't know—"

Fargo shook his head. "No, it wouldn't work. Need some catgut for this kind of sewing." He crabbed backward and got his spine planted against the tree trunk. Sitting up straight didn't ease the pain, but he still felt better.

Both women were silent, but not because they were out of things to say. They just seemed reluctant, so he prodded them. "What's on your mind, gals?"

Kristina looked at him, then at Minerva. She looked back at Kristina, then at the Trailsman, back to Kristina, and finally his way. The fugitive hemmed and hawed for a bit. "Mr. Fargo, we were wondering if one of those dead pigs could be put to use. Seems an awful shame to leave good pork sitting on the ground like that."

He shrugged. "What'd you have in mind?"

"Being as it's still Christmas Day, couldn't we make a roast out of one of them?"

Fargo shifted his back before answering. "Reckon we could." His eyes flitted across them. "Either of you know anything about butchering a hog? Because I don't know that I'm up to it."

They both looked disgusted at the notion. "Skye, my father is a hardware merchant, not a butcher," Kristina protested.

"I was a house hand, not no field hand," Minerva added. "Know how to cook one, but nothin' about what comes before that."

Fargo scanned the camp. One galvanized bucket was about all they had for holding hot water. That wouldn't come close to being big enough to hold a hog while its bristles got scalded off. Unlike most animals, the hog's skin was edible—that's what gave bacon its rind. But you could eat it only if you removed the bristles. And doing it that way meant you'd get all the bacon. You generally lost a lot of the belly meat if you just skinned the hog.

But then again, it wasn't like they were set up to smoke hams or cure bacon or render lard or put up sausage. They just wanted a rack of ribs or a roast for Christmas dinner, and maybe some meat to travel with for a couple days. Skinning the carcass would work fine for that.

Fargo smiled. "It's like this. Much as I'd cherish some pork roast tonight, I just don't feel up to butchering a hog. If you gals feel up to it, though, I'll tell you what to do. If you don't, we'll just say no more about it."

Minerva and Kristina wordlessly exchanged glances and grimaces. Eventually they nodded at each other before turning to him with their agreement. Both had cleaned chickens, geese, and the like, so they figured they could handle a hog.

Following his instructions, they found one of the smallest of his victims, a young gilt whose throat had been slit during the attack. With his rope tied around the back legs of the four-month-old female, they dragged the sixty-pound pig over to the next oak and tossed the rope over a limb.

Then they were just going to pull the carcass up.

"Wait a minute," Fargo cautioned. "You're going to be slicing the belly open in a few minutes. It's a lot easier if the legs are spread. First slit the legs, just above the hooves. There's a tendon in there, the hamstring. You want to grab a chunk of firewood and run it through the hamstrings. That spreads the legs. You tie the rope to the wood, and hoist that."

It took them considerable tugging, along with a few slips as the carcass thudded down, to get the carcass up after they got the wood slid behind the hamstrings. Since the women now blocked his low view of the hanging hog, the Trailsman gingerly stood, still leaning against the tree. The long gash immediately started to bleed—not a lot, but what seeped out was still worrisome.

Fargo turned his attention back to the pig. Flanking it and holding knives, the women turned to him with a "Now what?" expression.

"The rest is pretty simple. You cut a little circle around its . . ." Fargo sputtered to a halt. How the hell did you say "asshole" to a couple of women, one raised reasonably polite and the other religious?

Kristina came to his rescue. "Around the place where the stuff comes out?"

Relieved, Fargo nodded. "That place. Get the circle cut. Then tie it tight so nothing drips out. After that, you just slit down the belly. Do it real careful, though.

You don't want to nick an intestine. What comes out can ruin the meat."

They used one of the tatters they had cut from his pants for tying, and the rest went according to plan, until they reached the breastbone, where their knives halted at the tough brisket.

"You'll just have to work through that," Fargo advised. "It's slow cutting." It took them about ten minutes, but they managed. Now the hog hung open.

"Grab the guts and pull 'em out," the Trailsman continued. "Then peel off the hide. After that, you can cut off a ham or get some ribs, and that'll be Christmas dinner."

The women looked disgusted as they reached in and pulled. Kristina held the tied-off top while Minerva came out with a handful of bloody intestines. The Trailsman felt some warm dampness and looked down at his leg. More bleeding. He'd have to do something about that gash soon, or a lot of things could happen, and bleeding to death was about the most pleasant of the possibilities—grangrene and amputation, or blood poisoning and long fever, or permanent muscle damage and going through life with a game leg.

Stitches. Fargo gritted his teeth at the thought. But what could they use for thread? Wait a minute. Doctors used catgut. The Trailsman searched his memory. What the hell was catgut? Didn't come from cats, he knew that. Now it was coming to him.

Sheep intestines. Clean them out, scrape them, slice them into threads. Well, there was a pile of pig intestines right in front of him. Generally that part of the pig got used for sausage casings.

The notion of using those hog guts to hold his left leg together made the Trailsman feel a bit queasy. But then again, it wasn't like they had anything else handy. And it would likely do.

While Minerva worked the bristly hide off the carcass, he got Kristina to fetch him a bucket of water, and set about making his own sutures. Without any tool except his belt knife, the process took a couple of hours.

It was almost dark by the time his nose told him that

their shoulder roast, cooking on a spit over oak coals, was about ready to eat.

"Do we eat first and sew later?" Kristina wondered as they sat by the fire.

He looked down at that foot-long gash. There wasn't much light left. If he ate first, they'd be poking at his leg in the flickering and uncertain illumination of a campfire. Sunshine was better for that. Besides, how the hell was a man going to enjoy dinner if he knew that as soon as he put his fork down, somebody was going to start working a big needle into his hide?

"Let's get it over with. You've got the needle?"

Minerva held up the tentmaker's needle he carried for mending tents, bedrolls, saddles, and the like. It was about three inches long and curved in a half-circle. He handed her the improvised catgut strands. "You're doing the honors?" he wondered.

"Miss Kristina and I talked over that, Mr. Fargo. Being as I did sewing by the basketful back at Mr. Oakley's—"

Fargo interrupted her. "I saw those long calluses on your thumb and forefinger. Just take one stitch at a time, tie it—"

"Mr. Fargo, I didn't know how to cut up that hog. But I do know my sewing."

He laughed. "Fair enough. But do go over my saddlebags and get my sharpening stone. Let's shine up that needle a little."

Kristina came back with the stone, as well as a couple of the half-inch-diameter lead balls that his Sharps used for bullets. "Won't you want to chew on one of these, Skye?"

He sharpened the needle tip in a few strokes before answering. "Guess I'll see about biting a bullet. It may not hurt as much as we think it will."

"Please don't thrash around, Mr. Fargo," Minerva cautioned as she threaded the wickedly big needle. "Just hold still. This ought not to take more than a few minutes."

The Trailsman did chomp hard on a Sharps bullet when the point pierced his skin. But that was really out of habit. Sure, he was disgustingly aware of what was going on down there. But it wasn't as painful as he thought it might be, perhaps because things happened so quickly.

Minerva was fast and dexterous. It didn't take her much more than a minute, maybe even less, to tie a knot a couple inches back from the needle, jab the point in, cross the wound, and poke it back out. She'd pull it reasonably tight, Kristina helping by pushing the two sides of skin together, and tie it off. One slice with a knife to snip the leftover suture, and Minerva was back at it again.

Twenty minutes later, Fargo was contentedly putting some of that hog inside him. "You are a marvel with that needle, Minerva," he complimented, "and this roast tastes about as good as any I've had. Some men are going to be mighty lucky husbands someday."

"I've already got me a man," Minerva protested. "He went south and we're going north."

And Greta had been carried off to the north, except they weren't ever going to catch up to her. The only reasonable chance was finding some Comanchero and striking a deal through them with the Comanche. Except the Comanchero, as well as Greta, might be anywhere between here and Santa Fe, hundreds of miles away.

If they were lucky tomorrow or the next day, they still might find where the Comanche had cut away from this trail. But that wouldn't mean much. The time for trailing was past. The trick now was to figure out where they were headed, and get there.

The Trailsman reached for the jug and took a good pull. Damned if he was going to let all this fretting ruin his Christmas dinner. Not after he went through so much trouble to kill this dinner, not after the women had worked so hard at cleaning and cooking it. A man could always find something to worry about, anyway. Best to enjoy what could be enjoyed, and tackle the rest as it came.

This time of year, most places were real close to silent late at night. But since central Texas was fairly warm, even in December, the crickets never quit chirping and the frogs seldom shut up. Inside the tent, with

Kristina sleeping at his side, Fargo felt the hairs bristling on the back of his neck as he came awake. Some sound must have roused him, but he couldn't specify it. None of the outside noises sounded at all unusual.

Alert and tensed, he lay still. There it was, some deep heavy breathing. Maybe the horses. Movements out there. Well, hell, the horses were just hobbled, to keep them from wandering off very far. So they could be standing right outside the tent. No, the sounds of motion weren't the familiar sound of shod hooves. More like somebody padding around barefoot.

Fargo swore that the next time he camped in Texas, it would be inside something with thick walls, where he wouldn't be invaded by herds of swine, and now, whatever was out there. Of course, Tom's dogtrot house had fairly thick walls, and that hadn't done him a bit of good when the Comanche rode in. And back down in San Antonio, the Alamo had tremendous walls, which hadn't prevented Santa Anna's army from overrunning its defenders. So maybe walls weren't the answer.

Slowly and silently, the Trailsman stuck his head out the tent flap. His eyes were already adjusted to the darkness, so he quickly spotted Minerva, sleeping easily in a bedroll about fifteen yards away.

She really didn't have a right to sleep that easily. She was only ten feet away from one of the hog carcasses that still littered their clearing. It was curious that she'd lay her bedroll there. Most folks didn't like to sleep near corpses, human or otherwise. And that mound of dead pork was big. Three hundred pounds, anyway.

Well, no, it hadn't been there when she went to sleep, because the shadowy hog got up on its legs and started to shamble toward the center of camp. Since dead pigs hardly ever came back to life, Fargo figured he was looking at a bear in motion.

He cursed himself. This was stupid as hell, staying in the middle of all this fresh meat in bear country. He glanced over toward their butchering tree. A small bear, likely a cub, chomped away contentedly. At

92

least they wouldn't have to worry about burying the entrails in morning.

So there was Mama Bear and one Baby Bear. Papa Bear likely wasn't around, but there could be another Baby Bear. Fargo spotted him nosing around the pile of carcasses that he had used for a fort, only that morning. The she-bear was big, but not like a grizzly. Just brown bears, then.

What to do?

Nothing, he finally decided. You had to shoot a bear dead-on to kill it. Hitting that fatal spot between its eyes was chancy enough in broad daylight, let alone at night under starlight. No reason even to try unless those bruins gave up on pork and tried to start in on humans or horseflesh. He'd just have to watch, pistol in hand, until they threatened or moved on.

The east wasn't quite pink yet, but it was getting gray enough to blot out some of the dimmer stars before the bears shuffled out of the clearing, Mama dragging most of a pig. Fargo didn't begrudge her that, but he'd been through days that were more relaxing. Christmas sure hadn't been an idle day. He missed his sleep.

He was still trying to rub the sand out of his eyes when the smell of coffee drifted into the tent. While Minerva and Kristina chattered, he sat silently at breakfast. Maybe Christmas had been enough of an excuse to lay over for a day. Maybe not. The hog attack would have kept them from moving on, anyway.

But he could use his leg now, even though it smarted considerably whenever he moved it or even thought about it. His head hurt even worse when he tried to figure out what to do today.

They had to get going, if only so they wouldn't be camped amid rotting meat that would soon attract more bears, as well as wolves and coyotes. But where? Minerva certainly had good reason for wanting to head south, toward the border and her freedom. Kristina still felt somehow responsible for her big sister's abduction and would want to go north, since that's the way the Comanche had been riding.

Traveling solo, the Trailsman could have caught the

Comanche. His leggy and grained Ovaro was more than a match for their short-legged and grass-fed mounts. But it was too late now for that. And until he had any idea of why those German gents had tried to kidnap Kristina, he didn't dare leave her alone.

Something was missing in all this, and he was damned if he had any idea even where to look for the missing piece.

Kristina's voice drifted in, disturbing his thoughts. She sounded fairly cheerful this morning. "That was some Christmas, wasn't it?"

Minerva agreed that it had been, even if none of them had been around kinfolk.

Kristina said it had been a spell since her family had all been together, anyway. Not since her brother, Paul, had gone back to Bavaria a couple years ago.

"Why'd he do that?" Fargo wondered politely, hoping to take his mind off his worries. "Woman trouble? As I recall, he was a handsome fellow."

Kristina laughed. "The way it was told to me, he broke a few hearts when he left San Antonio, Skye. But I do not think that was the reason. I really don't know. Perhaps something to do with politics."

"Here or there?" Fargo prodded. He knew he was prying past the tacit bounds of politeness. But maybe he'd find out something useful. It couldn't hurt.

"Over there, I suppose. He is much older than me, Skye. When I was just a girl in the old country, he was part of a movement to make Germany one nation, a democratic one where people voted for their leaders, like the United States. Our father was also involved. Whatever they worked for, it did not come about. I think that was one reason our family came to Texas."

That tied with what little Fargo knew of German politics and history. There really wasn't a Germany over there. There were a whole bunch of principalities and duchies and the like, spread all over a chunk of Europe where most people spoke German. He'd run into enough emigrants to know that back in 1848, a big reform movement had failed. The governments there carried grudges against the idealistic sorts who had promoted reform. So many of the would-be reformers of Germany had come to America, where they felt more comfortable.

Minerva, of course, didn't feel all that comfortable in the United States. Couldn't blame her for that. But, at the moment, she wasn't worried about that. Instead, she glanced around at the dead hogs and speculated out loud. "Wonder what it was that set them porkers to running through here yesterday."

Maybe that meant something. Fargo wasn't really an expert on the habits of wild pigs. But a bunch of hogs, nosing around for acorns and pecans, wouldn't be likely to take off running, hell-bent for election and mean as sin to anything they met, unless they'd been alarmed. Tracking the herd's path wouldn't be much of a problem, and they couldn't have come from very far away.

"Guess I could head up their trail and find out," the Trailsman answered. "Kind of curious myself."

"But what about Greta?" Kristina fretted.

"Look," the Trailsman quickly reasoned, "we know that whoever took her headed this way. And we know that something around here scared those hogs into running through our camp yesterday. There ain't a lot of other folks moving through this country."

"So you think there is a connection?" she asked hopefully.

"I'm not too sure what to think," the Trailsman confessed, hoping that he wasn't grasping at a straw. "But it seems reasonable. Anybody have any other notions?"

They didn't, so within the hour, they were mounted and heading eastward, backtracking the herd of swine. The marks of their sharp hooves spread across thirty or forty yards. That meant that the herd had been truly frightened, because pigs, wild or domestic, liked to travel single-file.

The terrain was still up-and-down, but less heavily wooded than before. Earlier there had been unconnected clearings amid the connected stands of oak, mesquite, and juniper; now the trees were islands in a rolling sea of grass, brush, and cactus.

Down in a draw, not more than a couple miles from

where they had camped, the pig prints settled down. Rubbing his eyes and promising himself he'd catch up on sleep tonight, the Trailsman dismounted and looked closely.

Judging by the tracks and other sign, the hogs had been fairly settled here. There were depressions where they wallowed. Then, what?

Somebody had shot a pig, which would account for the hide over in the brush. Likely hadn't killed on the first shot. Just hurt it bad, so it started squealing hard, which frightened the others into scurrying off. And once a scared herd of any kind of animals, people included, began to run, just about anything could happen after that.

Fargo spotted the blood-splattered tree where the carcass had been hung, pretty much the way his own camp had done it yesterday. No meat remained. He forced himself to examine the entrails on the ground. No heart or liver in that festering, ant-ridden mess that he poked with a stick.

Indians liked organ meat, but their notions of hog butchery were a lot more informal than this. He scanned the little draw and figured the shot had most likely come from up ahead, then turned to the women to ask if they knew any folks that liked the hearts and livers of hogs.

"Goodness' sakes, no, Mr. Fargo," Minerva answered. "They fed that to us sometimes. Sometimes the only meat we saw from a hog was scrapple or chitlins. But if a body had any choice, you'd be eating side meat."

So these hog butchers likely weren't escaped slaves. He lifted his eyes to Kristina and saw that the wind had come up to toss her golden hair around her face.

"Many Germans consider the heart and liver delicacies," she explained.

But since most of the inhabitants of the hill country were German, more or less, that wasn't a lot of help. Yawning, Fargo remounted. The wind got a lot brisker as they climbed the draw. Up on the rise, he supposed he should feel grateful for the way it was making him feel more alert and awake.

Now, if he was riding along the reasonably wide trail up here—it might even be a wagon road—and spotted some fresh meat rooting around in that draw, where would he shoot from? Right over there, next to the brush. He told everybody to stay still, dismounted, and studied the tracks there.

More bootprints. Wide in the heel and toe. Like those he had seen outside Tom's cabin. And at the holdup of Kristina's stagecoach. Now the afternoon breeze felt chill.

Chill enough to make him totally alert. A pair of riders had come down from the north. They had halted here. One had fired several shots at a pig. Both had hunkered down the draw, cut it up, and hauled it back. So far, that made sense. But then they had gone back the way they'd come.

Maybe they were just local boys out hunting. But damn near every little farm here kept a few hogs in a pen. Why would anybody go to the trouble of hunting pork?

Travelers, like his own group? But then, why go back the way you came? Wouldn't you just move on once you'd brought down some dinner? And if it was only two men, the liver alone would have been dinner enough. They were hauling that meat to feed others somewhere.

Wherever that was, if it was nearby, somebody might have noticed something unusual in the past week. Any kind of hint would be damn welcome right now. Almost as welcome as sleep. But that could wait. He figured to head north for a while and see what he could see.

8

As the sun got serious about setting, its low rays caught the tremendous expanse of pink granite before them and made it sparkle, as though it had been flecked with gold.

The Trailsman reined up. He looked around as he waited for Kristina and Minerva to draw abreast. Right ahead, not more than a mile or so, it looked like the top half of a rounded boulder had just poked its way up through the rolling countryside.

Of course, they liked to do things in a big way down here in Texas. So the boulder was about two thousand feet high, and its base extended for at least a mile. As nearly as Fargo could tell, it was just one big bare rock with a bunch of peeled and slid-off slabs sprawled around its bottom.

Where the rock wasn't sparkling, it was the shade of a woman's blush, much like the exposed pink granite dome of Pikes Peak. The gigantic stone up there would have looked at home if it had been sitting a thousand miles away, up in the Rocky Mountains. Here it stuck out like a steamboat on a sandbar.

"Enchanted Rock," Kristina murmured as she pulled up beside him.

"You've been here before?" Fargo wondered.

Several blond curls rippled in the wind as she shook her head. "No. Many people do visit it, though. And there are many stories about Enchanted Rock."

Wide-eyed, Minerva turned away from the rock. "What kind of stories, Miss Kristina?"

The Trailsman had already heard most of the tall tales. Whenever men sat around a campfire after supper, there were embroidered stories about strange

98

places. Up by the Tetons, bizarre springs of scalding water, hot enough to boil an egg, with steam shooting up out of the rocks every so often. Over in Oregon Territory, gigantic, hairy manlike critters prowling the dense forests. In the Rocky Mountains, canyons so deep and so narrow that you could see the stars from the bottom, even at high noon.

Fargo prodded the Ovaro into proceeding. The path had widened in this more open country. They could all stay abreast, still following the return trail of whoever had shot the hog a ways back.

As they plodded along, Kristina told Minerva that one story had it that the Indians wouldn't go near Enchanted Rock. It made groaning sounds some nights, which frightened them.

Then she started another bit of lore and got flustered. She looked ready to cry when the Trailsman glanced her way. "What's the matter, Kristina?"

"We used to hear in San Antonio that . . . that back in the olden days when the Spanish held Texas, the Comanche rode into the town once and took a woman to Enchanted Rock."

"Peculiar, if they were really all that afraid of it," Fargo prodded. The tall tales you heard never did fit together. If the Comanche were frightened by Enchanted Rock—which didn't seem likely, since he didn't know of anything that scared the Comanche—then, why would they be hauling somebody to it?

"No," Kristina protested, "they were scared of the spirits that made the rock groan. So they were going to make a sacrifice to the spirits. That's why they rode into San Antonio and took a woman." She bit her bottom lip, which didn't prevent her from sobbing a bit as the wind carried off a few tears.

Her attack of grief was understandable. The Comanche had just taken her sister and ridden north afterward. For all that she or the Trailsman knew, the redskins had headed for Enchanted Rock.

That didn't seem at all likely, but Fargo sure couldn't come up with any good reason why Kristina shouldn't be fretting about such things, either. That was the trouble with worrying. Until you knew for sure what was going on, you just imagined things. And your imagination could get real gruesome.

They came upon the last descent stand of trees before the rock. A yard-wide creek babbled past the grove. "This is as good a place as we're likely to find for you two to stay the night," the Trailsman announced.

"Us two?" Kristina questioned. "Where are you going to be tonight?"

"Up on the rock," Fargo replied as he dismounted. "Might as well see if anything's been going on up there lately."

"But at night?" Kristina challenged as he helped her down.

"The moon's full, and it'll be up in a couple hours." He turned to hold Minerva's lean, muscular hand as she rolled out of the saddle.

"Mr. Fargo, you'd go up to that haunted place when there's a full moon? My heavens, you must be brave."

As he fetched the tent off a saddle and horse they had acquired from the estate of the late slave-hunters, he stifled his exasperation and explained the obvious.

"I'd be a lot braver if I wandered up into that bare rock under broad daylight." He found the hatchet and stepped over to lop a juniper limb and make some tent pegs.

Minerva mulled on that for a moment. "You mean you think there's some bad folks maybe hid up there. In the light of day, they might shoot at you before you could find them. At night, though, even with a moon, you could slink through the shadows like a skunk raiding a henhouse."

Fargo wasn't real fond of the comparison, but he smiled anyway and nodded. "Go to the head of the class."

"But what of us?" Kristina protested. "I don't want you to leave us here all alone. Not with roving bears and wild pigs and . . ."

He finished hammering in a tent peg before answering. "I don't like it either, Kristina. But look here. If things ran the way I'd like them to, we'd be sitting on your sister's porch right now, watching Billy pester squirrels with that slingshot while Tom showed off on the harmonica and we all sipped whiskey."

It was close, but Kristina hadn't burst out into full-bore gushing tears quite yet, so he crabbed over, grabbed another fresh-trimmed stake, and used his hammering to emphasize his points as he continued.

"This cussed world never does run the way we'd like it to." Bang. "All we can do"—wham—"is play the hand we're dealt." Thump. "The best we know how." Shit, damn, hell, fuck. Why in tarnation hadn't he known enough to look at the stake instead of at Kristina? His just-pounded left thumb would have to quit smarting someday, likely next year about this time.

The creek wasn't as icy cold as it ought to have been, but it did quiet his hurting thumb enough so that he could be of some use as they got the rest of camp set up. At least something had gone right. The wind had settled down, so they could get the tent up without a struggle. After dinner, as soon as a few of the brighter stars emerged, the Trailsman moved slowly toward Enchanted Rock.

Hoofprints led into the gravel at its base. So it seemed reasonable that the pig-hunters he wanted to find were now camped up in the granite massif. The horses would likely be tethered somewhere down here, amid the jumble of broken slabs, many of them fifteen or twenty feet high.

Find the horses first, and then find the men and start asking questions?

No. The Trailsman decided to stick to his original plan, working his way up this dome in darkness, by starlight. It really wasn't all that steep. If wet, it would be slick enough to cause problems, but that wasn't a consideration tonight. He would climb to the summit and then wait for moonrise.

A full moon would give him a tolerable view. He might even spot the tethered horses and get a good lead on where the men could be holed up.

Which could be about a hundred different places, if the stories were true. From what he'd heard, Enchanted Rock wasn't nearly as solid as it looked. Deep overhangs, hidden clefts, and even genuine caves were said to dot its flanks. One cavern supposedly penetrated for better than a thousand feet. And there was the usual tale of an ancient Spanish mine—lost, of course—that held more gold than El Dorado, more silver than Mexico, more emeralds than Colombia.

The Trailsman wanted to move silently, so he went barefoot, holding his boots in his left hand, leaving his right free for grasping—for a hold on either the rock or his Colt, whichever might seem needful. Sharp gravel poked at his feet until he began his ascent of the smooth massif.

It had sure looked smooth and bare, anyway. Once he started up, he was surprised at the diversity he found. Trees popped up where they had no rightful business growing, frogs croaked from little reed-rimmed pools.

Still warm with the retained heat of the day, the granite felt good against his naked feet until lichen scratched at his toes. Every now and again, a surprised lizard would surprise hell out of him, scatting over his feet. The first time that happened, Fargo reflexively kicked and almost lost his balance as the tiny shadow flitted off into the darkness.

Much worse than the lizards, though, was the cactus. No matter how carefully he stepped, his ankles still grazed against spines so sharp and long that they could stab through boot leather, let alone bare skin. No telling where those spines might be lurking. Stick your foot atop what just had to be comfortable solid rock, and your sole would get pierced. Each step had to come slow and thoughtful.

Fargo didn't see how he could get lost, even in this darkness, as long as he kept going uphill. He reckoned he had to be pretty close to the summit when he paused and looked east. The first hint of tonight's full moon was peeking out. He had timed it fine. Slowly, he headed toward the summit, hoping he'd get there before it got too light.

Up a few more steps, Fargo stopped again, frozen in his tracks. No wonder the Comanche thought an evil spirit dwelt here. A shuddering low moan rose from the earth beneath him. Like an audible fog, the mournful pitch enveloped Fargo. It wasn't the ground that was shaking, although it seemed that way at first. The ponderous bass note was pitched so that Fargo's innards vibrated in dismal harmony with these eerie notes.

Though warmth still radiated from the rock, Fargo shivered.

He reached the summit just when the full silver glow of the moon began to bathe the bald knob. Below him, Enchanted Rock continued to moan. He gazed toward the encircling horizon. Gaunt mesquite loomed. Other protruding bare rock massifs dotted the countryside. Fargo felt as though he had just climbed a monstrous tombstone in a long-abandoned cemetery.

Fargo peered back the way he had come. About two hundred yards away from where he had started to climb in earnest, the creek wandered into a jumble of boulders. It looked like a good place to put up some horses, but stare as he might, he couldn't be sure. Fargo thought there were motions in those deep shadows, but he knew from experience that a man's eyes could play cruel tricks. Stare long enough in a certain direction, with your mind set on seeing something, and sure as hell, you'd see it. Or think you did.

So he continued scanning around the base of the vast dome, slowly and deliberately. Over to the west the moon had just risen enough to bring a spot out of the shadows. Those were horses, sure enough. The texture of the terrain was softer, grass instead of gravel, indicating a pool.

It was hard to count the horses, hard to see them at all, unless they moved. He stared patiently, waiting for flicked tails and nodded heads. There were eight or nine, at the least, all unsaddled, if the pale one was any indication. That stood to reason. Folks didn't leave their mounts saddled when they settled in for the night.

Fargo's lake-blue eyes worked up the rock from the horses. Of all of Enchanted Rock, this shimmering stretch looked most barren. Under the full moon, it resembled the bowl of an upside-down polished silver spoon. For the longest way up from the bottom, there weren't any shadows, clefts, trees—no shelter of any kind.

But, no, Fargo realized, this face of Enchanted Rock wasn't really all that smooth. The moonlight seemed lustrous, but it wasn't bright enough to provide a true sense of depth. What looked like continuous smooth rock before him actually broke off for a cliff, maybe an overhang.

The break wasn't more than a couple hundred yards away. Now grateful for the wind moaning through this massif, because it might obscure any inadvertent sounds he made, Fargo edged down that way.

What made places like this good hideouts is what made them hard to approach. Coming up from below, any visitor would be in plain sight—and an easy target—for the better part of a mile. Peeking down from above, without a rope to belay yourself, was stupid. Working around and approaching from a side was the only practical way. But even then, the bare rock left you exposed.

The closer he got, the more cover Fargo found. The weathered granite that formed the overhang before him had broken off and tumbled down, to leave immense slabs and scattered boulders. Fargo worked through them, padding barefoot and avoiding the considerable temptation to curse when his toes met cactus spines.

Because the moon hadn't quite finished climbing over Enchanted Rock, the overhang was still shadowed, although that would change in a few minutes. The darkness rose about fifty feet above Fargo and extended for perhaps a hundred yards. He listened intently. Above the waning moans, there were the rustles of moving creatures.

Humans, he discovered, after sidling over for a better look into the recess.

Bathed in moonlight, two Comanche stood at the lip, about ten yards apart. They had to be sentries. Behind them was a jumble of robes and blankets—likely half a dozen warriors were bedded down here. They weren't what Fargo had been looking for—men who wore wide-heeled boots instead of moccasins with long leggings—but he'd settle for what he could find.

He watched their conversation in sign language. The shorter one, standing bowlegged on the left, was glad that the moon's light had finally reached them, so that they could pass the time without being so bored from staring out over a dark expanse of rock.

The taller Indian, using the lance he held for emphasis in his reply, answered that boredom wasn't nearly so bad as those terrible sounds from inside the rock. He'd have been a lot happier if they had just gone ahead and sacrificed the yellow-haired woman, so that the rock's spirit would be comfortable.

"But the Men from Across the Great Water give us many strong horses in trade for the yellow-haired woman," the short one shot back, his gestures quick and angry. He added something to the effect that they could easily please the Spirit of the Rock with another offering.

Since the sentries were shooting dark glances at each other during their silent argument, Fargo edged closer and made sure of his cover.

Now Tall Warrior, the one closest to the Trailsman, only fifteen yards distant, was pointing off to a shadowed area downhill and over toward the east side of the granite dome.

"This person still thinks," he signed, "that we all should not have traded with those Men from Across the Great Water. So far they have given us only two jugs of firewater for the woman. So far we have not seen the horses they promised. They are white men, so we should know that they never keep their word. They tell lies even when the truth would serve them better."

Short Brave responded emphatically. "Their skin is the same color, but they are not lying Americans," he pointed out. "The Men from Across the Great Water are from a different tribe. Are you so stupid that you do not remember the story among our people from many seasons ago when Men from Across the Water first made their camps here? And did not the Men from Across the Water bring us a pig to eat early today? They are not enemies of our people."

Fargo willed himself to remain motionless as he pondered on what he had just learned from the complaining sentries. The yellow-haired woman had to be Greta. Whoever the Men from Across the Great Water were, they had her in a cave close by.

Clambering directly on over to that cave was out of the question. Tall Warrior and Short Brave might not have been the most attentive sentries he'd ever encountered, but they wouldn't miss more than six feet of Trailsman scampering across bare rock in bright moonlight. But Fargo could work his way back the way he'd come, across the top of the overhang to get to the cave. Not that he would be sure of avoiding discovery that way, but the odds were better.

Once at the cave, he would have to play it by ear. But there was a damn good chance he could just sneak right in and get Greta out of there quickly and quietly, since her current captors could well be relying on these Comanche to do all the guarding tonight.

Making no more noise than a shadow would, the Trailsman edged back. His bare foot felt the scaly tail of a lizard. The critter jerked its tail out of the way and scampered into the rocks. In the process, it dislodged two or three pebbles, causing them to scrape and clatter.

Any lizard that clumsy sure as hell deserved to get plucked up and devoured by one of the owls that patrolled this countryside at night. But no matter how dead that lizard got, it wouldn't help Fargo. The Comanche sentries snapped to instant alert. Tall Warrior poised the lance as a bow and arrow materialized in Short Brave's hands. They peered intently across the rock.

Stay still, Fargo told himself. Stay goddamn still. Don't even breathe. Maybe they won't spot you. After all, pebbles and the like must scrape and clatter all the time around here. In a minute or two, they'll go back to bullshitting each other, and you can get your ass out of here.

But Tall Warrior's intense round face was staring

right at him. Fargo could tell by the wide-open eyes that the man had seen something.

How long could a man crouch without blinking his own eyes? Fargo wondered. For the rest of his life, he glumly realized. Which might be about twenty seconds. Less than that. The battle lance blurred as the Indian drew it back, and Fargo's mind raced.

Stay still, and maybe get pierced by it? But if it missed, then perhaps the two sentries would conclude that there wasn't anybody out here. Even at that, though, they'd come down to fetch it, and they'd be close enough to smell his presence then. Duck. And be relieved that he could finally move his aching leg as he came up shooting right after the missile whisked by, just where his shoulder had been.

Fargo dedicated his first round to Short Brave. Short Brave was farther away, but the closer one had already thrown his weapon, whereas Short Brave had a lot of arrows. He was just notching his third one, with two whizzing through the air toward the Trailsman, when the Colt bullet caught him square in his bare chest.

Short Brave's bow flew one way and his quiver the other as his arms flapped outward. He froze that way, rising to his tiptoes, before the bullet's slamming force finally toppled him backward, into the shadows.

With the shot, his taller companion rolled down flat. Fargo stepped out from his crack in the rocks. Since they could see him, he might as well see them. Seemed only fair.

Tall Warrior was crawfishing around, back by the blankets, trying to rouse the band. To provide some noise to help him out, Fargo snapped off a shot into the fluttering shadows.

It sailed low. The bullet smashed against the cavern's rock floor, then skipped, like a flat stone flung into a still pond. As a whistling disk of flattened lead, it continued on its way. Its sharp whirling edge sliced into Tall Warrior, a couple inches above his eyes. His head exploded in a mist that erupted from the shadows. Fargo suspected he couldn't have done as neat a job with a scalping knife.

But even as Tall Warrior reeled back, the echoing gunfire drew reinforcements.

From somewhere back there, arrows were starting to fly Fargo's way. As he scurried for cover, Fargo sent a couple more rounds back into the darkness. One seemed to ricochet harmlessly, although it doubtless made the Comanches thoughtful about coming forward. The other hit something satisfyingly soft. That, though, was about as much satisfaction as Fargo could enjoy as he sandwiched himself inside a crack in a fallen slab, barely wide enough to breathe in.

Damn. There were a bunch of them up in that recess. They had enough arrows, axes, lances, and the like to turn him into a pincushion if he ventured out from his newfound fort.

His shelter was solid enough. There had to be twenty feet of granite straight ahead, between him and the Comanche cavern. But all he'd have to do is sidle about a yard to his right, and he'd be an easy target. Through the opening that he had clambered into, Fargo could see most of the cave if he twisted his head and bent a little.

The Trailsman had one round left in his Colt. But there was time here, which he took, to make that six rounds. He had his belt knife, which was well-nigh useless at this distance. And of course the throwing knife, sequestered in the boots he still toted. But there was barely room here to scratch himself, let alone throw anything. It was strain enough to twist and bend to get his boots back on. He might as well wear them. No point in being quiet and stepping on cactus if the Indians already knew where he was.

If they ventured out, he could get them. And if he tried to leave, they could get him. They'd be more comfortable during the wait, especially if this standoff lasted through the night and into the heat of day. Besides that, trying to outwait Indians was playing the game their way. They were damn good at patience. Maybe better than he was. He really didn't want to find out. Playing the game your enemy's way pretty well guaranteed that you'd lose.

Low rustling sounds ventured into the Trailsman's

lair. More moans from Enchanted Rock? Maybe. No. This was picking up into a low howl. A breeze. Make that a regular wind. This afternoon's gusts seemed to be picking up where they had left off at sundown.

Fargo slowly brought his arm to his side and a finger to his lips. He wet it, then hoisted it on up, quickly stabbing it into the star-filled sky overhead. Even Comanche archers weren't likely to hit a quick-thrust finger, although Fargo could swear he sensed the breath of a passing arrow. But he also felt a decent breeze up there.

He stood in the rocks for a few more minutes as the wind above him picked up speed. Now some flotsam—cactus spines, dead leaves, and the like—was skidding along the smooth exterior before sometimes dropping onto him.

Good. That meant that the wind was fairly strong at its peak and that it was gusting. That might be enough to get him out of here with his scalp on.

Hat jammed down and Colt in hand, Fargo burst out of his cover. Just two Indians standing side by side up on the lip of their cave, both with bows, their notched arrows pointed toward him.

In constant motion, Fargo didn't aim real precisely. His first round whizzed between them as a steel-tipped arrow sparked the rock at his feet and another sped past his ear.

Fargo's second shot caught the left brave's shoulder, which released his ready arrow into a passing gust. Weakly shot, the feathered missile sailed off the edge of the dome, carried by the wind. And his friend's arrow, although aimed better and shot harder, likewise lost a battle with the breeze, eventually lighting on some rocks far away from Fargo.

As long as the wind was blowing, the Trailsman had the advantage. He used it to stop suddenly and take careful aim. A bullet to the neck sent the standing archer to the Happy Hunting Grounds. The other one was thrashing some on his back, arms and legs pawing and flailing.

Chary with his ammunition, Fargo didn't waste a bullet on him. Besides, there were two more warriors coming to the fore. A heavy lance flew straighter in this gusting wind than a light arrow did, but the man's aim wasn't quite as good as it should have been. A ball of lead from the Trailsman's Colt poked into the Indian's muscled belly moments after he cast the lance. He spun like a waning top, then stumbled to the edge, a hand-size hole spouting blood out his back.

The other warrior gave up on his bow and arrows. With a whoop from his throat and a wicked knife in his hand, he leapt from the cavern's mouth and zigzagged, in great leaping bounds, toward the Trailsman.

A fair fight would mean both using a knife. But just how fair had they been to Tom Baker? Fargo swallowed his bile and caught the moving target low, shattering the man's pelvis. His legs collapsed beneath him as he fell into a ball and tumbled on down the rocks.

Fargo didn't stand around and wait to hear what the bastard hit. He took long strides toward the cave where the Men from Across the Great Water were holding the Woman with Yellow Hair.

9

Heading downhill along the dipping dome of smooth granite, the Trailsman had to remind himself not to hurry. It was almost a certainty that Greta was being held down in that cave, two hundred yards away. The sooner he got there, the better. But one misstep could send him sliding on his belly down this immense rock. He'd be covered with scrapes and bruises. The spasms of pain rising from his stitched left leg reminded him that he really didn't need any more scrapes or bruises.

Fargo's catlike progress came to a hair-standing halt, anyway. No doubt curious about all the ruckus outside, a tall, lean man emerged from the cave down there.

A few precise but rapid steps put most of him behind a boulder. His shoulders and head remained visible. Unlike most men hereabouts, who favored wide-brimmed hats, this man sported a military-style forage cap, a low-crowned flat-topped headgear whose brim consisted only of a short visor in front. Standing ramrod-straight in the moonlight, he shouldered a rifle and began to scan the hillside through its sights. Any second now, the Trailsman would become his target.

Fargo waltzed sideways as the first bullet flew his way. The downhill rifleman's aim hadn't been all that good, because the round nicked the granite at least a foot from where Fargo had been standing. Long before the ricochet quit howling, the Trailsman had zigzagged into cover, a shattered sheet of rock.

In the process, the Trailsman got closer to the mouth of the cave and the man with the rifle. But it was still better than a hundred yards, too far for his Colt to be much good. Cursing to himself, Fargo reloaded the revolver while trying to keep his eyes on the rifleman.

The man was staring uphill, toward the Comanche overhang. Fargo glanced back that way. At its lower lip, two bodies sprawled in contorted positions that living men don't assume voluntarily. It was more than obvious that something had gone wrong.

The rifleman barked something quick and guttural back into the cave. His attention returned to his sights as the muzzle slowly panned across the Trailsman's refuge. Another bullet came Fargo's way. This one struck about a foot overhead. It was just happenstance that the flattened lead reflected away from him as it whirled off into the night.

Damn, Fargo muttered to himself. The way lead bounced around in this hard rock, there really wasn't such a thing as cover up here. He pulled his Colt up and sent two rounds toward the rifleman.

The problem with a pistol here wasn't power. Its charge of gunpowder could easily propel a lead ball that far, with more than enough force to kill. However, the short barrel wouldn't provide enough accuracy to matter. From this range, and shooting downhill at that, a pistol was about as useful as a peashooter.

But the rifleman didn't know that. At the sound of the first shot, he ducked low and stayed, even though Fargo's bullets skipped by harmlessly. Now the Trailsman felt more comfortable when he watched the jumble of rocks outside the mouth of the cave.

For what seemed an eternity but was likely less than a minute, all was still as silver light bathed Enchanted Rock. Then several forms stepped into the moonlight. Four of them. Also wearing forage caps, two closely resembled the hidden rifleman, toting the same long guns and striding like soldiers. As soon as they had moved out enough for a view, one halted. While the others proceeded, he brought up his rifle and began to swing it slowly back and forth across the rock above.

Fargo tried to ignore that and concentrated on the others. A rifleman stood in the fore, almost hiding another man. In the middle, a man had his arm across a woman's shoulders, pushing her along. The woman's hands were tied behind her. She had to be Greta.

In the silence of the night, some mutters from the

crouched rifleman floated up to the Trailsman. Before they could start shooting his way, Fargo sent down two more rounds, deliberately wide. There was too much chance of wounding the woman if bullets started bouncing around anywhere near her.

That halted their progress, but for only a moment. The hidden rifleman and the rear man began to get serious about sending lead up Fargo's way. And as they fired, the other rifleman, along with Greta and her escort, began to scramble down the dome. Greta may not have been of a mind to hurry, since the man beside her grunted harshly at her and then poked her side with the muzzle of his pistol.

They were slipping away. Fargo couldn't do much more than look, and even that was chancy, the way that the two riflemen were firing. They weren't hitting anything besides bare rock, but they weren't wasting lead, either. Their plan was to pin Fargo down until the others got away. Then the two rear guards could cover each other as they worked their way free.

Fargo looked at the Colt in his hand and realized that it would never be enough to disturb their plan from here. He had to escape and get down the granite and free Greta. At close range, he at least had a chance. From this distance, he was just a spectator.

Maybe not. He rolled down, out of view from below, and bellied along for several aching yards. At his fingertips was a chunk of rock, about the size of a man's torso. He pushed at it. He could sense that it was loose, not part of the massif. But it was sitting comfortably and not about to move.

Fargo snaked himself closer. In the process, his legs must have come into view from below. Two more shots roared from the rifles below. One grazed his right leg, burning like a hot iron as it left a gash. The stitched wound on his left leg, now being ground against the granite shards, sent up a searing pain, just to remind him that a sensible man would have spent tonight in a bedroll.

As they were reloading below, the Trailsman jammed his feet against something solid to give himself some leverage as he pitted his muscle against the rock before him. It began to move. Not much. An ant was about the biggest creature that might have been impressed by its ponderous, almost imperceptible progress. Its grating sounded loud to the Trailsman, but not nearly so loud as more gunshots in the distance.

Fargo crabbed to the side as the cover before him began to slide away, gaining velocity. It still wasn't going fast enough to notice from below, especially since the riflemen's eyes were fixed on him. Fargo sent a round downhill to give them something new to be mindful of.

They hunkered down. Another round from the Colt kept them there. They were sitting targets for four hundred pounds of sliding granite. It picked up speed as it approached their perch. Any second now, it would arrive near the cave's mouth with shattering force. Heavy chunks of rock would be flying every which way. Even as it struck, the Trailsman eyed a second candidate.

It wasn't as big, and it wasn't as square. Its corners had been rounded off, the way granite often weathered. With just a nudge from his foot, it took off downhill as an exhilarated Fargo forgot how much that kick had made his leg hurt.

Still scurrying, he rolled to his belly and scanned for more likely rocks, either for cover or to roll downward. There was one ten yards off. He fired downhill and started to rise.

His right foot was stuck. Had he wedged it in some crevice? He spun his head.

Damn certain his right foot had been caught, not by rocks, but by a wounded Comanche. The same bastard who had sailed downhill from the overhang had somehow survived both the fall and the bullet that had smashed his pelvis.

Behind the Indian extended a path of spattered blood toward the rocks where he had landed. He must have come around, and with a stoicism fueled by anger, he had pulled himself, hand by hand across yards of rock, to catch the Trailsman, whose attention was focused elsewhere.

Fargo kicked and tried to twist his leg loose. But it

wasn't moving all that well, on account of the bullet graze, and the husky warrior had a grip that a vise might envy, a grasp that he strengthened with his other hand.

The Trailsman started to bring his pistol around. The Comanche responded with a savage twist that made his ankle pop. The force of rotation traveled up Fargo's body and he could barely hold on to his pistol, let alone get it in into position to shoot this maniac at his feet.

Despite his strained efforts to bend upward so he could see what was going on, the Trailsman's torso fell back. He tried to cushion the fall, scrunching so that his shoulders, rather than his head, struck the granite first. But that just made it all the worse when his head snapped back.

Fighting to retain consciousness, the Trailsman struggled to lift his head. The Comanche's talon hands gripped his calves, and a probing thumbnail dug into the stitches on his left leg. His denim trousers hardly dulled the vicious force that found a tender spot and pressed and twisted.

Kick and wiggle as he might, it just made things worse. His boots were jammed between the unyielding granite and something that felt almost as solid, the Indian's barrel chest. Fargo tried to sit up so he could use his hands or arms or a knife or his pistol, but the wounded brave dug in harder and twisted more, and Fargo landed flat on his back. Straining every muscle, he could not lift himself more than a few inches before the pain and force sprawled him back.

The Comanche crawled up Fargo's body, bear-hugging his way toward something vital. Just the thought of how it might hurt when the brave reached his balls made Fargo shudder all the worse.

Roll, Fargo's instincts demanded, although it was hard to say what would happen or where they would end up. But just about anything had to be an improvement. Fargo holstered his Colt and stretched his arms out. On the downhill side, the Trailsman jerked in his right arm. He pressed down with his uphill left hand while twisting his torso.

The top half of his body began to roll over, but down at his legs, nothing was happening except blinding pain. No, the weight was shifting. Fargo was on his side and sure his backbone would pop out, but now there was motion down there. His legs and the Indian were starting to roll downhill, too.

With gravity on his side, the Trailsman put more intensity into continuing his motion. Grunting, he gritted his teeth and twisted violently. One side of Fargo's chest found the rock. Now the other side. He was flat on his belly, although his legs still thought he was on his back.

No matter how much power the Comanche could summon above his waist, the warrior's legs were useless. He could hold the Trailsman, but he didn't have enough leverage to keep the momentum from shifting as the Indian's belly rose. Nor could he prevent himself from beginning to slide down the granite slope.

Since Fargo wasn't of a mind to accompany the warrior, he grabbed at a rock. But it merely came loose in his hand as his shirt untucked and slid up. Fargo's bare flesh scraped across bare rock. As slowly as they were going, that wasn't too bad, except for a pincushion cactus that planted a bunch of spines near his navel.

That hurt enough, but the cactus hadn't slowed them down worth mention, either. Fargo and the Comanche weren't sliding any faster than a man could trot, but that was enough for Fargo's exposed belly to start heating with the friction as the cactus spines clawed in deeper.

If the Comanche would just let go, the Trailsman felt confident he could halt. But the bastard's grip didn't relax as they plunged, gaining speed as though they were going down a playground slide. Belly to the rock, Fargo plummeted feetfirst. The only consolation was that when they hit something, the Comanche would absorb the brunt of the shock, since he was below Fargo, still gripping the Trailsman's legs.

Slow fires burned at Fargo's chest, pain that won some strong competition with the spasms from his legs. About two inches from his eyes, fresh blood formed a dark trail in the moonlight. Was it from his scraped flesh? Had his leg wounds started acting up again? Was it from the Comanche's gaping wound in his loins? Maybe all of them. He couldn't tell. All he could do was slide downward blindly and hope they stopped before his belly got ground-opened.

Fargo couldn't hurt any more than he did now, anyway. No, he could. They started across some washboard ruts, ripples in the granite that bounced the Trailsman's torso up and down, slamming his tender scraped skin against the rock before lifting him with a jerk and starting all over again.

Comanche torture had earned its infamous reputation, but Fargo doubted that the brave at his feet was enjoying this any more than he was. The grip seemed to be slackening, but that might be just because the warrior's fingers were getting worn away by the granite.

They stopped abruptly with the sound of something soft, like flesh, being squished into something hard, like solid rock. Still facedown, Fargo couldn't see anything except the blood trail beneath him, but he thrashed his legs moments after impact, and felt them swing free, finally rid of the warrior's rigid grasp.

Ignoring how much it hurt to even think about moving, the Trailsman rolled onto his back and sat up, bringing his Colt up.

A chest-high wall, extending for several yards on either side, had stopped them. Enchanted Rock was like a half-peeled onion, with pieces of some layers still remaining, and this was one of them. The Comanche was jammed at its base.

Fargo doubted that the warrior had lived through this. His bloody rear end pressed into the little wall. He was doubled over, his shoulders pressed against his moccasins, but his head had snapped back so that he was gazing up at the moon, his braids trailing down his back.

As he caught his breath, Fargo stared intently, looking for motion. Nothing moved. But it hadn't been all that long ago that he'd figured this Indian was a goner, and yet the warrior had managed to creep up on him. Fargo slid down a bit and looked closer.

The man was dead. Still holding the Colt in his right hand, Fargo extended his left hand. Although the man's flesh was still quite warm, he'd been dead for several minutes. It wasn't the impact that killed him. He'd died sometime during that slide down the rock, but maintained that death grip in his effort to take the Trailsman with him.

Fargo exhaled slowly. No matter how hard a man was trying to kill you, you had to respect that kind of dedication.

The way he hurt, he could join some Indians in chanting that this was a good day to die. His legs pounded and felt like hot needles were twisting within them. But it was his chest and belly that pained him most. From neck to belt, the Trailsman was one long raw scrape. Under better light, he might have been able to find a chunk of skin that hadn't been rubbed off by the granite. But under the moon, it was all a blood-dark sweep of raw meat.

Without thinking much about it, Fargo struggled to his feet, untangled his shirt, and pulled it down. The soft flannel stung his skin like a scourge. Sporadic gusts of tonight's breeze grated the shirt against him.

The expansive wound would have to get washed and covered, the sooner the better. But first, Fargo had to figure out where he was. And he'd better get some idea of where they had been headed with Greta before he returned to camp and got himself tended to.

Fargo stood about twenty yards below the cave where Greta had been. Its dark mouth looked like a blemish against the smooth dome. The riflemen were gone. Fargo sidled over to where the footing was better, and figured that was the route they had taken.

Once on their path, Fargo halted and stared ahead. There was still a hundred yards or so of Enchanted Rock before the countryside took over. The Comanche horses had been off to his left. Where would the white men have kept theirs?

It had to be a spot where Fargo couldn't have seen them from the top, or he'd have noticed them. But from where he stood, Fargo couldn't decide just where that might be. So he began to search.

The front of his shirt was damp with blood before he was sure of their route. The horses had been over to his right. The gravel over there had been disturbed, and fresh piles were apparent.

Sudden noises to Fargo's right, around behind the dome, caught his attention. Feeling weak and dizzy, the Trailsman pondered momentarily whether to hurry over and chance making himself a target, or to move slowly and maybe get there too late.

Fargo hurried. The concentration that was required to keep his feet under him sometimes allowed him to ignore the blazing jolts of pain that started just above his ankles and welled up through his chest. Two gunshots made him move even faster.

Now he could see the action came from a nearby grove—the grove where the women waited. Shrieks and grunts, along with the whinnies and snorts of perturbed horses, carried on the night air.

Shooting into the trees would be foolish. For one thing, they were at least a quarter-mile away, well out of range. For another, he might get lucky and hit something—one of the women or one of their horses.

Riders emerged from the trees. Fargo took a deep breath and tried to simmer down. What was going on? No, they weren't riders, just horses. His midsection shining in the silver light, the Trailsman's Ovaro led the way, scampering out of the trees.

Now came riders. The lead man was one of the riflemen. He got out a few yards and covered as others moved from the tree shadows into the moonlight. Another rifleman charged behind him. Then Greta rode out of the shadows, still tied as she squirmed on the saddle. Almost next to her, but a pace or two back, came her guard. Just behind him was a second mounted woman, likewise tied. Kristina. Then another rifleman, who took up the rear guard as the others began to ride south.

Shooting at them would just waste a bullet and needlessly endanger two women. Maybe three. What had happened to Minerva? She wasn't with them.

Fargo started to holster his Colt, but snapped it back up and ducked when the rear rifleman, still star-

ing at Enchanted Rock, sent a bullet toward the Trailsman. Hoping that his shot would send the man on his
way so that he could get on down without being shot
at, Fargo returned fire.

But the rifleman stayed put and fired again. The
round whistled by, not a yard from Fargo's head.
Crouched as he gripped the pistol butt with both hands,
Fargo calculated how much his bullet would drop and
at the tricks the wind might play in that distance.

He estimated well. His round punched the man's
shoulder, forcing him to drop his rifle. As the rifleman
sagged in his saddle, his mount began to skitter around.
The Trailsman dispatched another bullet. It grazed the
horse's rump. The frightened critter reared and tossed
the man out of the saddle, then took off after the
others.

The downed man lay still as Fargo clambered down
the rock. But then the man began to crawl toward his
rifle, which lay almost within reach. The Trailsman
snapped off a round and hurtled himself forward.

With only one bullet left, Fargo scrambled closer to
have a sure shot. From this range, a man with a rifle
had the advantage.

At the foot of Enchanted Rock, Fargo had to stop.
His breath was coming hard, and he hurt like fury
every time it came. His legs protested vehemently
about being forced to move. He still had a quarter-
mile to go before he'd reach that rifleman.

The man was trying to be coy about sneaking an
arm out toward the rifle. Wishing he had his Sharps
carbine, Fargo sent out his last bullet, then whistled
for the Ovaro. A lot of things had to go right during
the next thirty seconds.

His big pinto cantered toward him as he swiftly
reloaded the Colt's cylinder. With the last ball rammed
into place, he swung aboard bareback and sent another shot toward the downed rifleman, just to keep
the man from thinking this might be easy.

Any second now, the rifleman might figure out that
he could go ahead and grab the rifle, because someone
shooting on horseback from a distance with a pistol
wasn't likely to hurt him. And once he had that rifle,

he could either shoot Fargo or knock the Ovaro down. That would keep Fargo at a distance.

Every bouncing step that the Ovaro took tore at Fargo. He felt as though some big bird was pecking at his chest while clawing at his legs. He had to cover that ground before the man got the rifle. Another snapshot forced the man to pull his arm back. But the arm was flung out again and the man had his rifle.

Riding bareback without a bridle, there weren't a lot of ways Fargo could persuade the Ovaro to turn suddenly. Leaning low, Fargo dug his knees into the pinto's flanks and pushed his mount's head hard with his left hand. The horse got the message. He veered to the right as the sprawling man ahead brought the rifle to his wounded shoulder.

But now Fargo was only thirty yards away and the distance was melting. It was getting difficult to swing that rifle around quickly enough. This was pistol range, and Fargo had the pistol. The rifle fell into the dirt, an instant after a round from Fargo's Colt burrowed into the man's clean-shaven face, just above his nose.

Damn. Not that the Trailsman had much choice but to kill the rifleman, but still, it would have been nice to be able to ask some questions.

A lot of it had already come together. These Men from Across the Great Water had to be Germans, from how they talked. There was a group of them— these men and maybe some others—who had made a deal with the Comanche to kidnap Greta.

The torture of Tom and the murder of Billy likely hadn't been part of the bargain; the Comanche just threw that in for good measure. Anyway, Greta had been taken, and the Germans met the Comanche at Enchanted Rock to make the trade.

So she'd been kidnapped. There'd been an effort to swipe Kristina off the stagecoach. And now the Germans had chanced across his camp, where they'd discovered Kristina. So they had her, too.

But why? That gnawed at the Trailsman. What was the point in all these kidnappings? Down in San Antonio, the Gottliebs were comfortable, but hardly wealthy.

If you were stealing people and holding them for ransom, there were victims who'd pay better.

It didn't make much sense. But there had been another woman here when Fargo left at sundown.

"Minerva?" Fargo called out as the Ovaro walked toward camp, skirting the body.

Some low groans and moans answered him, so he hailed again.

"That you, Mr. Fargo?" she eventually mumbled.

"What's left of me," he grunted as he rolled off the Ovaro, Colt still ready. He sure hoped Minerva was the only person left here, but he couldn't be certain.

Reeling and pressing a palm to her forehead, she walked dizzily toward him.

"You by yourself?" he wondered, his gun sweeping around.

"Think so. A body can't be sure. I just come around, Mr. Fargo. They knocked me cold with a pistol butt." She rubbed at the growing bump on her head.

Fargo found himself sagging into the ground. It took a lot of effort just to sidle his rear over to where he could lean his back against a tree, but he managed. "What happened down here?"

Minerva settled next to him before replying. "We heard the ruckus up on the rock, Mr. Fargo. It scared me awful, and Miss Kristina too. But finally she got curious and stepped out of the trees so as she could maybe see. Next thing you know, those riders pounded by here. They grabbed her and they grabbed me too. I hollered and clawed at them, and then one clubbed me. Last thing I knew till a minute ago. Kind of surprised to find myself still here."

"Still at the campsite," Fargo consoled.

"No, sir, Mr. Fargo. Still on this here earth."

10

By light of day, the Trailsman felt like hell. That scampering on the rock sure hadn't improved his stitched-up leg. Despite the salve Minerva had applied, his chest and abdomen stung from being rubbed raw along the granite. Kristina had been kidnapped right out from under him while he was almost within reach of Greta.

None of this was making much sense, and the dead man outside the grove wasn't telling any tales. He was likely German, considering the cut of his boots and that his small-caliber breech-loading rifle had been crafted in some town called Essen.

Fargo had already learned that much. Any further information would have to wait until he found someone to translate the papers he'd found in a button-down shirt pocket.

While Minerva scurried around, picking up camp before he started packing, the Trailsman stared bitterly into his morning coffee. Like as not, those papers were just bills of sale for horses or the like, and even if he knew what they said, the knowledge wouldn't do him any good.

The essence of tracking wasn't following a trail. Almost any observant sort could do that. What had earned Skye Fargo his reputation was his ability to think like his quarry, to put himself in another man's shoes and determine where that man was going, and why. Once you had that figured out, often you could be there waiting.

"Mr. Fargo, it's time to load the horses." Minerva's nagging barely disturbed his reverie. He rose mechanically and proceeded through the familiar motions: loading bags and panniers, testing their balance, assembling and covering the center loads, throwing the diamond hitches and snugging them tight.

All the while, the questions preyed on him while the answers stayed hidden.

From atop her mount, Minerva took her bearings after looking back at Enchanted Rock and toward the sun, low in the east. "We're headed south now, ain't we? Toward Mexico maybe?"

The Trailsman nodded. "Maybe. Main reason we're going south is because those riders headed south last night."

She pointed to the fresh impressions in the dirt. "That's their tracks, sure enough. Can even see which horse was being rode double."

"What do you make of all this?" Fargo wondered. Like all womenfolk, Minerva and Kristina had talked with each other, a lot more than they had talked with him. Maybe she'd have some notion as to why this gang of Germans was so intent on taking the Gottlieb girls.

"Miss Kristina seemed plumb horrified by what happened to her sister's family," Minerva began.

"She wasn't the only one that felt pretty disgusted by that Comanche raid," Fargo prodded, wishing that his belly didn't hurt every time he spoke or even inhaled.

Minerva scrunched up her lean face and looked thoughtful for a minute. "Miss Kristina was about as mystified as us about the rest, Mr. Fargo. She wondered why anybody'd bother to rob a stagecoach, just to grab her. She didn't think she'd ever done nothin' to upset nobody like that. Then her sister got taken by them savages."

"But the Comanche didn't keep Greta," Fargo reminded. "Instead of hauling her out to Comanche territory, they swapped her to those Germans for some horses. Or they planned to, till we showed up. I doubt any of them are in any condition to ride now."

Minerva chuckled. "I'd reckon not, Mr. Fargo. So it must be them Germans that're behind all this."

Fargo nodded. "That sounds likely, being as they

have both women now. But where are they taking them, and why?"

The lithe black woman glanced at the trail and assured herself that the Germans' tracks were still before them. "Mr. Fargo, they don't dare be seen much in the open with those women, do they? They're in about the same fix I was when I was running away by myself, ain't they?"

"Hadn't thought of it that way," the Trailsman confessed. "Been hurting so much, and so damn mad, that I guess I haven't been thinking much at all. But you're right. They would be staying low. You can't ride around in broad daylight on well-used roads with two tied-up, gagged women and not attract some attention. With this full moon, they'd likely travel at night and set up dry camps until they get where they're going. They'd sure want to hurry through this open country. Once they got into some wooded land, maybe ten miles ahead—that must be where they're holed up now."

Minerva's brown eyes flicked at the rise looming ahead of them. "If they was just fixing to kill them sisters, they'd have done it by now, right? So the Germans must want to keep them for something. Now, when I was on the run, I figured that when I found my own kind, I could rest up for a bit—nobody'd notice me there among other black folks. Riding with you, I kind of stick out."

Fargo looked ahead and saw they were almost to the top of the rise. "That you do, Minerva. But it doesn't bother me if it doesn't bother you."

She laughed, low and hearty. "Not at all, Mr. Fargo. Only thing that bothers me is that I ain't yet got to Mexico to be with my man in our own little house. I don't even care if it's one of them mud houses. Just so long as it's ours."

Atop the rise, Fargo paused to let the horses blow. He was getting quite a string behind him, more horses than he really wanted to care for. When they got to a town, it'd be a good idea to sell the extras. There were times when money was more useful than horses.

Now some of the finest horseflesh the Trailsman

had ever seen were coming his way—two companies of U.S. cavalry. Army mounts generally tended to be practical, but this was prime Kentucky horseflesh. One company's forty steeds were matched browns; the other's were all grays.

It had to be a detachment from Fort Mason, headquarters of the Second Cavalry, the army's crack outfit. For some reason, the Second got the best horses, officers, and soldiers. Fargo stared closely at the advancing patrols. The guidons, little flags carried by the leaders, indicated the grays belonged to Company A and the browns to Company G. They were still a considerable distance away in the vastness that sprawled before him.

He turned to Minerva. "Just in case anybody asks, you're my slave, and we're headed for San Antonio after buying some horses hereabouts."

"But, Mr. Fargo," she protested, "that ain't how folks with slaves travels. You'd bring along a man to help you, not some wisp of a gal like me."

"Shit," he murmured to himself, thinking quickly. He lifted his voice. "Okay, then you ran away from my place just south of San Antonio, and I came up here and caught you. Bought some horses while I was at it."

She nodded glumly. "Well, okay, Mr. Fargo. But the Good Book says we ought not to bear false witness."

"Look, you are a runaway slave, Minerva. And it's the army's bounden duty to enforce the laws, which means returning you fugitives to your owners. You want to go back to Mr. Oakley's while I rot in some Texas prison for helping a slave escape?"

Her tight curls shook around her ears. "Say no more, Mr. Fargo. I see what you mean, master." They started downhill at an easy clip. If all went well, they'd do no more than greet the soldiers, but it sure didn't hurt to have a story ready if all didn't go well.

The guidons passed them, one company on each side, with no more than waves from the soldiers. But once the leaders of the patrol had passed, they were amid the main body of cavalry. And it was there that a lieutenant motioned at Fargo. The serious expression in the man's long, bearded face indicated that there would be trouble if the Trailsman didn't stop.

"Good morning, sir," the lieutenant offered in a Kentucky drawl. "Fine day to be riding, isn't it?"

Fargo nodded. "That it is." Might as well get this over with. "Something on your mind, Lieutenant?"

The officer nodded. "There have been reports of Comanche in this vicinity. Can you tell us anything?"

"There were six of them roaming over Enchanted Rock last night. I think I got them all, though."

His eyes mere slits, the lieutenant scanned Fargo, Minerva, and the horses. "All six?"

"As best I know. In the moonlight, it's hard to be certain."

"And with Comanche, you're never certain."

Fargo nodded agreement. "Sounds like you've seen a few."

The lieutenant nodded. "I have." He looked hard at Fargo again. "You resemble a man I've heard of. You wouldn't be Skye Fargo, the Trailsman, would you?"

"Depends on who's asking," Fargo answered. "And you'd be?"

The officer moved his sleek brown mount closer to the Trailsman, so that there was a chance of shaking his offered hand. "Lieutenant John Bell Hood, commander of Company G."

As they shook, Fargo recalled a few stories. "You led that outfit on a big sweep back in '57, didn't you? Five hundred miles into Comanche territory?"

"And only nineteen savages to show for it." Hood smiled. "But you do what you can to keep order along the frontier." Hood's expression fell. "So there were six up at Enchanted Rock. Maybe there's more nearby. They've been raiding to the south—burned out a farmstead about ten miles out of Fredericksburg."

"I know," Fargo said softly. "They were friends of mine."

Hood shrugged and inhaled deeply. "So you followed them up to the rock. Well, Fargo, I'm glad we stopped to talk. Knowing that will change our plans for this patrol. We can swing to the west and mayhaps catch up to a few more before they get too far away."

"Hope you do," the Trailsman encouraged. "Time for us to head on south, I reckon."

Hood nodded, then stopped, his face grim and frozen. "Those horses. Where'd you get them? And that black woman. Where's she from?"

"It's a long story," Fargo evaded, "and you did seem to be in a hurry to catch up to those Comanche."

Hood mulled for a moment. "Look, Fargo, those horses belonged to some slave-hunters that disappeared a few days back. We got some descriptions back at the fort. Now, I don't know if I hold with slave-hunting or not, but it is a lawful activity. And murdering folks sure isn't. So I'd sure like you to explain where you ran across those horses."

"I knew you would." Fargo's eyes flitted, confirming what he already knew. He and Minerva were surrounded by soldiers. There wasn't hope one of getting out of here. No, maybe he could persuade a horse to rear, and if the confusion spread, they just might break away from the twenty armed men nearby, all trained soldiers in a crack outfit. But shit, even if they did, there were eighty men on this patrol—enough men and good horses to run them down, no matter how fast and hard they tried to ride. And there wasn't cover around here worth mention.

Hood interrupted his dismal thoughts. "Well, Mr. Fargo, I await your answer. For somebody surely slew the men aboard those horses and then took the horses. And I do hope it wasn't you, but I must know."

"What happens if it was me but there was good reason?" Fargo hedged.

Hood's low mouth lifted a bit. "In that case, the disposition would be up to our commanding officer."

Fargo recollected what he knew of the Second Cavalry in Texas. "Colonel Johnston, over at Fort Mason?" Mason was a good thirty miles to the west, a tedious detour. Maybe it was time to tell the whole story and see if he could get on with his pursuit of the Germans. Hood was a dedicated cavalry officer, sure enough, but he looked like a man who might listen to reason.

Hood shook his head. "Mason's still the headquarters of the Second. But they just reactivated Fort Martin Scott, right outside Fredericksburg. That's where the old man is now. And Johnston got transferred. Colonel Robert E. Lee's in command now."

Fredericksburg. That's where they were bound anyway. Or close by. The Germans had to be hiding out thereabouts with the captive sisters. That's one place where the men wouldn't stick out or cause much comment, even in a gossip-ridden little town. And for certain, Fargo could get those papers translated by somebody in Fredericksburg.

It wasn't like they had much choice except to go along with the army, and if that would get him closer to where he was headed anyway, so much the better.

The worst that Lee could do, after hearing his story, would be to turn Fargo over to the civilian authorities. And since most of the folks in Fredericksburg were opposed to slave-hunters and slavery in general, likely not much would come of it. There was the time factor to consider, but hurrying after Greta's captors hadn't done much good yet. So maybe it was time to quit being in such an awful rush.

"Okay," Fargo conceded. "We'll go down to Martin Scott and explain things to Colonel Lee."

A trooper's outstretched hand appeared and Fargo surrendered his Colt. Moments after Hood had issued orders in a soft voice, they were headed south again, escorted by four troopers.

Fargo noticed that Minerva had the same idea he did. Like him, she kept her eyes on the Germans' tracks, and when they left the road, a mile or two outside Fredericksburg, she looked over and nodded. Other than that, it was a tedious ride. Like all soldiers, the cavalry troopers bitched about their duties and their pay, thirteen dollars a month for privates. But they seemed to think highly of both Hood and Lee.

Inside the ramshackle log structure that served as headquarters of this off-and-on fort, Lieutenant Colonel Robert E. Lee rose to greet them as an orderly escorted them into his office, late in the afternoon.

"Skye Fargo. After hearing so much of you during

my tours of duty in the West, it is indeed a pleasure to meet you." Lee's soft Virginia voice was courtly as he turned to Minerva. "And you would be Miss Minerva?"

She nodded, and Lee's deep-set eyes sparkled in his bearded face as he turned back to the Trailsman and motioned for them to be seated.

"Mr. Fargo, as you are well aware, it is my duty as an officer of the United States to see that the laws are duly enforced." He exhaled sadly. "And there were inquiries made here, only several days ago, as to the whereabouts of certain gentlemen from Arkansas. They seem to have vanished from the face of the earth, although their horses are accompanying your party. Perhaps you could explain?"

Fargo leaned back. "I'd hardly call them gentlemen, Colonel. They came upon us and fired first. What was I supposed to do with their horses?"

Lee chuckled. "That stands to reason. But I will need confirmation." He turned to Minerva. "Miss, did you witness that?"

She nodded hesitantly before answering. "Indeed I did, sir, just like Mr. Fargo tells it. They up and started shooting first."

Lee settled more comfortably into his chair. "Good. That's all I needed to hear. You won't mind if we hold those horses here, will you, so that their relatives might claim them?"

It sounded more like an order than a question, but the horses hadn't been of much use anyway, with just the two of them. "No problem there, Colonel. Anything else?"

Lee leaned forward, his arms on the desk. "Mr. Fargo, I know there's more to this than what I've been told. Now, you can tell me or not tell me, as you deem appropriate. But I would very much appreciate hearing the entire story, and I give you my word of honor that it will not leave this room without your consent."

"And what happens if it comes up that maybe a law or two got bent some?" Fargo wondered.

"I believe our constitution provides a protection against self-incrimination, Mr. Fargo." Lee smiled. "And I know that a man of your reputation isn't likely to be just wandering around the hill country. There's more to this than meets my eye."

Fargo mulled for a minute. He and Minerva could just walk on out of here. But Lee would be suspicious as hell, for good reason, and that certainly couldn't help. And if he told Lee the whole story, maybe the officer knew something that would help the Trailsman. Fargo figured he could skirt the part about Minerva's arrival, and they could both pretend it hadn't happened.

The Trailsman explained what had happened since he'd ridden away from Tom Baker's house, a few days before Christmas, to pick up Kristina at the stage station.

"So these Germans, whoever they are, appear to be abducting members of one family," Lee said, settling back in his chair. "And they put the Comanches up to that raid on the Baker place." He pondered a bit longer, his eyes closed. "You know, Mr. Fargo, as tense as the political climate is in our own nation, what with that awful talk of secession and that insurrection at Harper's Ferry that I was called to put down when I was back East this fall—perhaps there's something political at the root of this."

"I'm not much of a hand at figuring out politics, Colonel." Fargo shifted uncomfortably in his chair. "Fact is, I think I'd rather track Comanche than have to study politics."

Lee nodded. "I'm in agreement there, Skye. But it wasn't our nation I was thinking about. Could this be somehow connected to events over in the German principalities and duchies? There was a democratic uprising over there in '48, which sadly failed. But the agitation continues, I've been told, and hard feelings must certainly linger on both sides. People everywhere seem reluctant to let bygones be bygones."

Fargo recalled what Kristina had said of her older brother, Paul. He and their father had been active in that movement. And Paul had gone back to the old country. He leaned forward. "There might be something to that, Colonel. I've got some papers from the German guard I shot. Maybe those would tell us something. But I can't read German."

Lee commiserated as he leaned back. "I'm glad there was a translation of Clausewitz when we studied his work at West Point. But there are men here fluent in that tongue." He raised his voice and summoned his orderly inside with instructions to fetch Sergeant Braumstetter.

"As for the kidnappers, Skye, you're sure they're holding the women close to town? And you know where their trail departs from the road?"

Fargo rose and stretched. "It's nigh dark outside, which means they'll be moving soon. Toward town, perhaps, or to some place where they feel safe. This is wooded country, hard for cavalry. Much as I'd like to have the army on my side for a change, I just don't see that mounted soldiers would do much good."

Lee sighed as he, too, rose and shook his broad shoulders. "I suppose you're right, Skye. And it's a good way to get captives killed if you ride in with soldiers. But I want you to know that if you should need the assistance of the Second Cavalry in this matter, it will be gladly offered."

"I'm glad to hear that, Colonel." Fargo glanced over at Minerva, who sat there demurely. Behind him, the door opened, and Sergeant Jacob Braumstetter reported in, apologizing for his odor and disheveled appearance. He'd been cleaning stables.

Heavyset, clean-shaven, and dark-haired, for several silent minutes he pored over the four pages that Fargo had found.

"I would guess that this is a letter they planned to post," he announced. "But it makes little sense, in German or in English."

"How's that?" Fargo wondered.

"From the sound of it, they were on a scientific expedition. At least they said they found the bird they had been looking for. But they complain that the old bird would not sing for them. They planned to find its nest and get another, in hopes that the new one would sing. The Indians have been most helpful, though, in their search. And once they hear the song, whoever's getting the letter will know what to do."

"It took four pages to say that?" Fargo probed.

Braumstetter shrugged. "There were many formalities in the text. I could read it word for word if you wish."

Fargo looked at Lee, who obviously shared his interpretation. The Germans here were working for some people back home. The kidnapping of Greta and then their lucky abduction of Kristina were indeed tied to something on the other side of the ocean. What was it that Greta hadn't sung about?

Her brother's whereabouts, maybe. That made sense. If Paul had once stirred things up in one of those tight-run kingdoms, he might be at it again. Except he'd be in hiding this time around. And it might be easier to get his family in America to tell his whereabouts than it would be to find him in Bavaria or Saxony or wherever.

"No, I reckon that's fine," the Trailsman told the sergeant, who laid the papers on Lee's desk and turned on his heel, toward the door. Then he spotted Minerva, stared at her, and turned back.

"Colonel, sir," he barked.

"Yes, Sergeant?"

"That woman there. She's an escaped slave from Arkansas. She fits the description perfectly that I read over in the—"

Lee raised a hand, palm out. "I am aware of that, Sergeant. I commend you for your alertness. But the situation is in hand. After all, Mr. Fargo here is the Trailsman, who tracks down and catches many fugitives."

Braumstetter shrugged and stepped out the door.

With those sad, deep eyes, Lee looked up at Fargo. "Skye, if you and Minerva can arrange to leave immediately, my command here would be greatly simplified." He paused until he was sure Fargo had caught his drift. "Good luck on finding the abductors of those women," he added.

Fredericksburg sat less than three miles from Fort Martin Scott, but it was near dark when they arrived. Fargo planned on putting up for the night somewhere and then nosing around in the morning. Somebody must have noticed those Germans, and if nobody had, he could head out in daylight and follow their trail. One way or another, he'd find them, along with Kristina and Greta.

The respectable hotels would hardly rent a room to him and Minerva, no matter how innocent their relationship, so the obvious place to stay was Tom and Greta's Sunday house. They stabled the horses so as not to attract attention with their small herd, and risked discovery by firing up the stove for dinner. But the bright moon hadn't risen yet, and Fargo left the windows shuttered so the lamplight wouldn't spread into the street. A decent hot meal felt good, and a hot bath would feel damn near as good. But Minerva was not only married, she was something of a prude. Fargo debated on leaving her for an hour or so and going downtown to find a tub with hot water at a hotel.

"Mr. Fargo, I could sure use a chance to clean myself," she murmured as she settled into her chair, comfortable from dinner.

"Wouldn't hurt me a bit, either," he agreed. There were a couple rooms here, and if she wanted to continue being so modest, it was likely they could work something out. "Tell you what. You find some pots and get them onto the stove. I'll pump some water outside and bring in the buckets. You can go first."

She smiled. "That's considerate of you, Mr. Fargo. Mighty considerate." She rose and began to assemble pots on the stove.

When Fargo returned from his third trip to the pump, a full oaken bucket swinging in each hand, he damn near dropped them. Shimmering in the soft glow of the coal-oil lamp, a naked Minerva stood between the stove and the tub. And she didn't look at all embarrassed, either.

11

The astonished Trailsman came close to giving the plank floor a thorough washing that it really didn't need, because he almost dropped the two full buckets. He stepped back suddenly, felt them sloshing, and set the pails down before looking up again.

"Is something the matter, Mr. Fargo?" Minerva's small but firm breasts, her hardened nipples dark points, bobbed pleasantly. The soft light from the lamp gave her a bronze hue as it played across her smooth skin. Fargo's eyes moved down across her flat belly and slim hips, pausing at her lush and curly pubic hair. He continued to savor the view as he moved on down to her lithe but muscular thighs.

"Nothing wrong, really," he muttered. "It's just that this comes as a bit of a surprise, considering how shy you've been, along with all your talk about what the Good Book says." He forced his eyes to move over to the kettles on the stove. "You sure you know what you're doing here?"

"Sure, Mr. Fargo. While you was out pumping water, I thought it all through."

He gazed at her lean face while her eyes moved down his chest, toward a bulge that was growing in his Levi's. "I reckon you know what I'm thinking about right now, Minerva. What I want to know is what you're thinking."

She tossed her head back and laughed, her voice still low and husky. "Well, Mr. Fargo, I got to thinking that it's sure hard to make your way through this world without sinning something powerful. Why, if you hadn't borne false witness, I'd be on my way back to Mr. Oakley's. And if you hadn't killed, we'd all be

135

dead. Land sakes, I hate to think just how many of the Ten Commandments you've broken."

"You do what you have to do," Fargo replied, wondering if she hadn't peeled off her clothes just to make sure she had his attention while she delivered some sort of religious lecture.

"Point is, Mr. Fargo, it just ain't fair or right if you have to do all the sinning that it takes to get done what ought to get done." She stepped toward him and placed one hand on his shoulder while the other moved beneath the buttons of his shirt, those strong seamstress fingers kneading and soothing his scraped flesh.

He nodded, keeping his arms at his side as he reined his desire to embrace her and pull that warm body against him. "Minerva, you've got a man. A man waiting for you in Mexico."

"What he don't know won't hurt him," she murmured as her nimble fingers undid shirt buttons. Her other hand found the area between his shoulder blades and did its best to erase the tension he kept trying to keep there.

Fargo mulled for a moment, then gave a monstrous shrug. "Well, if that's the way you see it, I sure won't be the one to tattle." His shirt was undone and the supple hand on his back was now under the waist of his trousers. He lifted his arms and embraced her. To his chafed chest, her undulating breasts were better than any salve.

For a minute or more, they stood clutching each other. A waft of steam from the stove reminded the Trailsman that he still hadn't finished his errand.

"Let's get this water heating," he suggested, "so it'll be ready when we are."

That taken care of, they settled atop his spread-out bedroll. His shirt had vanished in the process. His jeans were about to follow, as soon as Minerva managed another couple buttons on the fly. That might be a while, though, since she'd found something a lot more interesting than buttons for her hand to play with.

"Mr. Fargo," Minerva whispered, "I'm just a runaway and you're such an important man. Those soldiers all knew you. I'm a nobody. I tried to steal your horse. But you've been so nice to me. I got to do something nice for you."

A wave of tension surged up in Fargo's back. If he'd been built like a cat, his hair and beard would have stiffened and bristled.

"Minerva, you're not a nobody. You're a human being, just like the rest of us. And you don't owe me anything. So, if that's why we're here, let's stop this now before you do something that you won't feel right about, come morning."

He began to roll away. Sure, it'd be more than fun right now, but if a tumble tonight meant a weeping, angry woman at his side tomorrow, he could forgo the pleasure. Not happily, to be certain, but he liked to think he'd learned a few things about women over the years.

Minerva's hand found his shoulder and tugged. "Mr. Fargo, can't we . . ." Her voice caught. "Can't we just be friendly here, and do what comes natural when a man and woman be lying down without their clothes on, and pleasure each other some?"

The Trailsman relaxed and rolled back to her side. "That's exactly what I had in mind."

"You got too much on your mind, Mr. Fargo."

Before he could mutter a protest, her lips had smothered his mouth, and her tongue, lean and muscled like the rest of her, sparred with his, joining and probing.

Meanwhile, she wrestled his trousers and balbriggans off, the clothes sliding away leisurely as they lay side to side. His hands traced along her back to the swell of her heaving rump. The throbbing tip of his swollen shaft explored the moist thicket, which billowed to and fro with delectable pressures and tantalizing brushes.

Minerva twisted her head, indicating she'd like to stop kissing for a bit so she could catch her breath. Fargo didn't mind, seeing as there were those shapely nipples so close by.

"Mmmmm, Mr. Fargo, you sure know what to do to make a gal feel good."

He slid his top hand down her rump, pressing

smoothly all the way. His probing fingers found her damp cleft. She writhed toward him, increasing the welcome sensation with more of her smooth flesh crowding against his yearning manhood.

He paused in the midst of switching nipples. "Minerva, you seem to have more than a fair idea of what a man likes best."

She giggled. The tremors moved in little waves that lapped at his rigid shaft, almost like caresses, while her hands, firm against his lower back, drew him even tighter against her.

Pressing against her this way felt good, but there were sure as hell ways to feel even better. Without much leverage, but with the force of considerable desire, he rolled Minerva onto her back.

As if they were a great oiled machine, he found himself right in position between her spread thighs. His organ seemed to have a mind of its own as it found that moist cavern and began to enter.

Minerva, too, seemed to be running with a mechanical energy that thrust up her hips. Despite Fargo's mass, she came up smoothly to envelop him, aided by her muscular legs and the feet she had planted flat on the bedroll.

The Trailsman met her thrust with his own, plunging even deeper, enjoying the sweet soothing pressure that seemed to envelop all of him. Not just the shaft that yearned for more, but every bit of him was submerged, from the head that had lost its worries about Comanches and Germans, through the raw-scraped torso that no longer ached with every breath, past the sliced leg where the stitches seemed to have vanished.

"You're a marvel, Mr. Fargo," Minerva whispered between feverish pants. "A marvel." Her hips rose again, like a windswept wave.

He plummeted ever deeper, helping them both with the pressure applied by his hands on her arched rump.

"You mean there's more?" she gasped in mock alarm.

Fargo answered in the most convincing possible way.

"I want it all," Minerva panted. "All, all, all."

His hands came out from under. He swept his arms

back, hooking a knee with each elbow. Still stroking smoothly, he swung his arms forward, so that her knees were hooked, more or less, on his wide shoulders. Minerva was now coiled, her weight on her shoulder blades, her body in direct line to absorb him.

Fargo kept his own weight on his knees and planted hands, sliding in and out as her desire built. "Mr. Fargo," she whispered, "now."

He smiled down at the writhing woman in his shadow. She couldn't see the smile, because she had her eyes closed as her head rocked in rhythm with his slow and shallow thrusts. "We'll get there," he assured her. "We'll get there. But it's just plumb foolish to get in too big a hurry."

Between hurried breaths, she repeated her earlier observation that he thought too much. "Just do what seems natural here, Mr. Fargo, just do that."

What seemed natural was to rock back, moving his weight to his knees as he moved his hands to her hips. When he shifted forward again, all his force was concentrated in his midsection, a powerful surge whose swift progress could be read in Minerva's ecstatic face.

Once she had the idea, she cooperated for a dozen or so more long, deep strokes. But there came a time when a man ought to get in deep and stay there. They both knew when it arrived, because her internal muscles clamped on a deep stroke.

Withdrawing even a little bit seemed out of the question, and Fargo was right where he most wanted to be, anyway. He exploded, deep inside her. If he hadn't felt himself shuddering, he'd have known anyway by the frightful way she began to get even crazier beneath him, even as she grew tighter around him.

With a lusty, triumphant howl, she too arrived at her destination.

Even after they'd settled down a bit, they were still lying close by each other, atop the bedroll. The steam boiling off the nearby stove was almost a bath in itself, but it did seem foolish to have gone to all that work to take baths and then not bother to.

He began to sit up.

"Mr. Fargo, you're not leavin' me, are you?"

"Just enough to put some water in the tub," he advised. "Might as well take baths, being as we're both all dressed up for that."

Minerva laughed. "I suppose. But I think I'd like it if that tub was big enough for the both of us. You ever try anything like that, Mr. Fargo?"

He grabbed a pot and poured the steaming water into the galvanized tub before replying. "Minerva, you were just saying I did too much thinking. Must be catching. What I might or might not have done when I was sinning in the past isn't all that important right now, is it?"

She sat up, glaring a bit before a dreamy look settled in. "Reckon that's so, Mr. Fargo. But I surely do want you right next to me, and with that little tub . . ."

Fargo emptied another pot. "Where there's a will, Minerva, there's generally a way. I reckon I'd enjoy soaping you, and I bet you wouldn't mind returning the favor. And we could figure out the rest as we went along."

She brightened as he returned his attention to the tub. Damn. He'd been so astonished to walk in on a naked Minerva earlier that he'd heated all the water. Nobody likes to be boiled alive, and he wasn't of a mind to stand around and wait for the water to cool.

The only thing to do was to take the wooden buckets back out to the pump for some cold water for mixing until the bath was at a comfortable temperature. He mentioned that to Minerva before he peeked out the back door. The moon was just starting to come up, so it was likely too dark for anybody to get disturbed by the unexpected sight of a tall broad-shouldered man, his chest still a maze of scabs and scratches, standing out there bare-ass naked, running a pump.

Like all pumps, it squeaked, and tonight it seemed to howl, worse than those dying pigs had. Or maybe it was the evening chill. It could have been that he didn't feel all that comfortable walking around without clothes. But for whatever reason, the Trailsman didn't like the sensation and felt more than relieved to get back inside, where a hot bath would cure his overwhelming case of goose bumps.

Minerva had been thinking about ways they could have fun in and around the little tub. Maybe not. Could be it just came natural to her to straddle it while the Trailsman sat inside and worked his tongue up her ebony thighs.

That was before she wiggled atop his lap, leaning back against his angled legs while sliding her feet over his shoulders. He barely even noticed how cold his feet and calves felt, dangling over the edge, or how the rim of the tub worked against his back.

As clean as he could get, and pretty well spent, the Trailsman should have slept soundly. But he found himself waking later with a start. He scanned the room, every nerve alert. Such moonlight as had seeped in revealed nothing out of the ordinary.

What, then, had awakened him and made the hairs on the back of his neck feel so prickly? He felt edgy, the same way as he had when he'd been outside naked, running the handle on that noisy pump.

Sounds. Minerva breathed easily next to him. Once in a while, something would pop inside the cast-iron stove, and he could even hear the soft whiff of air entering its firebox. Nothing outside. No, there was something, like cloth rubbing against something rough, perhaps a limestone wall or the slab wall of the privy and shed in back. Footsteps, too, maybe?

At times like this, a man could convince himself that his own heartbeat was the sound of an advancing buffalo herd. It was best to have a look.

After grabbing clothes and dressing carefully in the darkness, the Trailsman padded to the rear of the house. Opening the door just a crack, he peeked out into the moonlight. Back by the privy was a slab-walled shed that held firewood and had stalls for two horses. Fargo glanced around, but returned his gaze to the shed when its side door opened and two men stepped out.

They weren't exactly shouting at each other, but they weren't whispering, either, so he could hear most of their conversation. A cold knot gripped his belly when he realized that it likely wouldn't do him much good to hear their talk, since they would almost certainly be muttering in German.

To Fargo's surprise, they spoke in English. "I'd say it's a certainty that he's in that house," the shorter and seedier one explained. "There's no horse in the stable, but somebody's in the house, since there's smoke coming out. They said they saw him at the stable." He stuffed a snuffed-out candle into the pocket of his patched coat.

The taller man, whose clothes weren't as shabby, lit a cigar before answering. "Much as I'd like to see him now, I guess we'll just have to come by first thing in the morning and talk to the Trailsman then."

His companion glanced up at the stars. "Won't be all that long till sunup, Mr. Oakley. Couple hours. But I guess I can manage if you can."

Oakley. That was the name of Minerva's owner. But, hell, there could be a lot of Oakleys. Sure. And it was just some coincidence that someone named Oakley was working so hard to find someone known as the Trailsman.

"We'll have to," Oakley answered as he began to stride down the alley. "I've tried every other way to recover that runaway wench, and nothing worked. Truth is, even if she's a fine seamstress, she's not worth this much trouble. But it's a dreadful example to the others when one gets away and isn't brought back. So I'll hire the best."

"From what I've heard, Fargo is the best. He reads sign better'n the Apache, they say. Reckon that if anybody can track down a fugitive, it'd be him. Glad I could help you find him, Mr. Oakley."

Their voices trailed off, but Fargo waited until the sounds of their boots striking gravel were indistinct before moving on out the door. Hiring on for Oakley to find Minerva would be about the easiest money he'd ever made, and it would be lawful money, too. But damned if he'd take it.

Fargo debated leaving Minerva a note and decided against it. She'd said she hadn't been taught much reading, and he had to move quickly now anyway. He pulled on his socks and boots, then stepped swiftly out the front door.

In the silvery moonlight, Clement Oakley looked more than surprised to find the Trailsman waiting for him at the front door of the Nimitz. Especially when the Trailsman knew his name.

"Good evening, Mr. Oakley. Or maybe I should say good morning. I'm Skye Fargo. I understand you wanted to see me."

Oakley, who was almost as tall as Fargo but considerably rounder on account of a paunch, gulped hard a couple times before meeting Fargo's outstretched hand with his own. "My, my," he finally stammered. "I just hear that you're in this town, and you pop up out of nowhere to stand right in front of me. You are good."

Fargo nodded. "It's my business to find people from time to time. But I don't really read minds. You want to explain your proposition?"

Oakley shivered and drew up his coat. "Wish we could sit down over a bottle first." His eyes moved up and down the silent, empty street. "But nothing's open. Want to come up to my room?"

Fargo shook his head. "No. Explain your business first, and if I decide we've got something to talk about, then we can get comfortable."

With a look of resignation, Oakley shrugged. "It's simple enough, I suppose. I grow cotton just across the Sabine, over in Arkansas, with about forty hands, mostly field workers. Every now and again, one runs off. Generally we find him. Last summer, one field hand ran off and hasn't been found yet. His wife was a skinny thing, did our sewing. And last month, she took off, too. I want her found."

"Not the man?" Fargo prodded.

"That's been so long ago that he's either dead or escaped to Mexico by now," Oakley muttered. "There's still a chance with her if somebody good gets on her trail. And you're good."

"The best isn't cheap," Fargo reminded, accepting Oakley's offer of a cigar. The warm smoke would feel ood, and the longer he could talk to Oakley, the better.

"I'll make it worth your while, Fargo."

"I'm sure you will." The Trailsman glanced toward the east, where some gray was replacing the black, obliterating the dimmer stars. "Just out of curiosity, though, what happens after you get her back?"

Oakley shrugged. "I'll have to make some kind of example out of her, lest the others get such notions. Then I'll sell her, so as she won't remain as a bad influence."

"I see." Fargo pulled at the panatela to make sure it would stay lit. "But I reckon you don't tell the new owner about her rebellious ways."

The planter laughed. "Not unless he asks. It's like most other business. A man ought not to tell flat-out lies, but there's no sense telling any more truth than is needful."

"Reckon that's so," Fargo agreed. "I've got reason to think she passed through to the north of here in the past day or two. A slip of a gal runnin' away, all on her own, isn't likely to make much time. So it shouldn't be hard for me to catch up to her shortly. Can you stay here at the Nimitz for a couple days?"

Oakley nodded. "Certainly."

"Then do it. If I'm not back with her before you decide it's time to return home, leave word there as to how I find you."

Oakley pulled his right hand out of his coat pocket, and they shook on the deal.

By now, it was getting almost light out, at least by comparison, and there were some stirrings down at the livery stable. As Fargo had suspected, Oakley's guide last night was the night man at the stable. And if the man was so talkative and helpful for Oakley, it seemed reasonable that he'd extend the same courtesies to the Trailsman. But a little smooth talk wouldn't hurt.

"Pretty good piece of work, figuring out where I had to be staying."

At the sound of the deep voice above him, the rumpled hostler lifted his head out of a hay pile and tried to blink himself awake. He was still at it when Fargo continued.

"Turns out that I could use a little local guidance, too." The stable hand sat up. "You got a name?" the Trailsman asked.

"Cantwell. Buck Cantwell."

"Okay, Buck, there's some German gents hereabouts."

Buck rolled his blue eyes. "There's always lots of them hereabouts, Mr. Fargo."

"Hear me out. Tight group, maybe half a dozen or so, showed up in the past couple weeks. Speak no English, or precious little, anyway. They brought guns from the old country. But they didn't bring over their own horseflesh. So maybe you can tell me something."

Buck balled up his fists and rubbed his eyes as his face grew pale. "I don't know nothing 'bout that, Mr. Fargo." He began to stand, but collapsed back into the hay when the Trailsman's boot hooked his ankle.

"What'd they say they'd do if you told anybody about them, Buck? They came in at night, from the back, didn't they? They paid you well for some horses, considerably above the going rate, and you passed on the regular price to the boss and kept the difference, right? What's going to happen if you tell me all about it, Buck? Are they going to turn you over to the Comanche, or handle the dirty work by themselves?"

Buck had managed to curl up, but he was still shaking enough to make the entire pile of hay quiver around him. Fargo tapped his butt with his boot. "Now look up at me, Buck, and give me a civil answer before I have to get rude."

With what looked like an awful strain, Buck sat up. "You won't tell them I told you nothin', will you?"

"I don't figure on telling them anything," Fargo intoned, his hand perched on his Colt just in case Buck couldn't figure things out from the serious tone of the Trailsman's voice. "Did it happen the way I've said?"

"Pretty much," Buck conceded. "But I don't know their whereabouts. Honest, Mr. Fargo, I don't."

"Now, Buck, don't be so hard on yourself."

"What?"

"You seem to know pretty much everything that goes on around here. I just can't imagine that you'd be so ignorant that you wouldn't at least hold a notion as to where those German gents might be holed up."

Fargo didn't think it was possible, but Buck managed to shake even more. His Adam's apple bobbed and he kept licking his lips, as if his mouth was drying up. "Couple miles east. Top of a draw." He continued with some reasonably explicit directions to a farmstead. Every time he faltered, his eyes fell to Fargo's Colt, and he found the inspiration to continue.

Somebody up front started to holler that he wanted a horse and buggy, so Fargo figured this conversation had gone on long enough. "Go tend to your work now, Buck. I can fetch my Ovaro myself." Fargo began to walk away from the hostler in the hay, then turned. "If I got the wrong directions, my friend, I'll be back to talk to you some more."

Buck slowly clambered to his feet, all the while assuring Fargo that there was no reason they'd need to resume this conversation. Outside, a goodly portion of Fredericksburg was stirring, so Fargo left the Ovaro tied to a hitching post downtown and walked discreetly to the Bakers' old Sunday house.

The way things had been going lately, Minerva would be gone. But, no, she was just sitting up in the bedroll with a worried, dazed expression that turned to surprise when she saw him step before her. He told her there was food enough inside for several days, and to stay inside during daylight and not to go any farther than the privy at night. As soon as he added that a Mr. Clement Oakley was in town, staying at the Nimitz but apt to wander just about anywhere, she was in enthusiastic if hushed agreement with his orders.

Within the hour, as the sun got around to making a formal appearance a couple of miles east of Fredricksburg, the Trailsman recognized several horses in the pole corral a hundred yards below him. He allowed himself a smile at the realization that Buck had given him good directions.

He'd have to get up close and figure out who was there. Then come up with a way to break out Greta and Kristina and keep their captors from coming after him. That might have to wait until darkness fell tonight. After that, he would have to get back to town and somehow settle matters with Clement Oakley without returning Minerva.

Just thinking about all that lay ahead of him made Fargo tired, so it was time to do something. In the long shadows of morning, he made his way easily down the brush-spotted hillside to the cabin in the valley. Made of local stone and fairly substantial, it was still a dogtrot, split into two halves.

From about fifteen yards away, where the homestead clearing started, he edged around slowly. There had to be a way to make this work to his advantage. Men's voices, muffled but still harsh and guttural, drifted his way, as did what sounded like Greta's and Kristina's. They were on the south end.

Good. The brush came closer there, giving him enough cover to get within a few paces of the stone cabin. There was a window, but it was just oiled paper, so he couldn't peek inside. Besides, it was too high to see through from where he crouched.

Fargo strained forward, just to be sure, and heard something rustle behind him. He spun on his toe, his hand coming up with his revolver. A man's legs were right before him. Something tremendous exploded, just inside and above the Trailsman's left ear.

12

Sharp jolting spasms punctuated the dull but ponderous ache that throbbed incessantly inside the Trailsman's skull. Even the most trifling motions, like blinking his eyes or twitching his mouth, set off thunderous roars. His chest felt like somebody was raking it with hot needles. A moist sensation, low on his left leg, advised him that he was bleeding down there by his stitches. Straight-backed wooden chairs never offered much comfort anyway, and they got a lot worse when you had your hands tied behind your back and your own legs laced to the chair's.

Fargo felt bad enough, but his pain got even worse when he opened his eyes again for another look at Greta, sitting across from him in this small, dim room. Her matted blond hair flew every which way, her face bore swelling plum-colored bruises, what remained of her dress was soiled and tattered, and what showed between the facial bruises and the top of the dress was even worse. Just below her neck, a crimson line, an inch wide and populated by oozing blisters, stretched for about a foot between her shoulders. Something long and red-hot, perhaps a fireplace poker, had been pressed against her and held against the woman until her pale flesh sizzled.

Greta sat so impassively that Fargo wasn't sure she was conscious, so he said, "Howdy, Greta. Fancy meeting you here."

She attempted a thin-lipped smile and gave up on it before answering, her voice a whisper. "They caught you too, Skye?"

What in hell did she think? That he'd just dropped by because he'd heard they were having a party here?

He shook his head to clear off the irritation and was rewarded by what felt like a sledgehammer in each ear, taking turns as they pounded. "Looks that way," he finally grunted. "Don't remember much of it."

She gasped and started to sob with a trickle of tears. After a moment she controlled herself and her round face lifted. "What can we do, Skye? They have Kristina, too. What will they do to her?"

Fargo gritted his teeth and tried not to look at Greta's recent scar. Instead, he gazed at her pale-blue eyes. "Greta, I'm not sure I know what's going on. I'll tell you what I think, and you tell me if I'm wrong."

She nodded. Fargo slumped back, relaxing as best as he could, while he sorted out what he'd seen and what he'd been told.

His wrists were tied snugly with a rawhide thong—tight enough to keep him from doing much, but not so tight as to cut off circulation to his hands. As he spoke, he wriggled and twisted.

Not that he had much hope of working free, but it beat not trying. His holster was empty. But jostling his right foot around brought a familiar pressure against his calf, so he figured his throwing knife was still in its hidden sheath, part of the leg of his boot. He didn't have any way to reach it, but at least he knew where it was.

"Okay, for some reason, these Germans want to find your brother, Paul, who's over in the old country agitating against the Elector of Hanover or the King of Prussia or whomever."

She nodded, so he went on.

"And the government couldn't find Paul there, so it sent some agents to Texas, where Paul had family. The idea was to get you or Kristina to talk about where he was, who his friends there are, that sort of thing. Then they could go back to Germany with enough information to bust up this conspiracy against the government."

Just saying that much was an awful effort. Fargo felt the sweat building up on his neck and trickling down his arms. He could also feel that his hands were still shackled, and that he hurt in a lot of places that he hadn't noticed before.

Greta nodded. "That is what they wanted." She

149

stifled a sob and bit her lip. "But I don't know much about all that, and Kristina knows even less. My parents would more know. So why did they take us?"

More sweat beaded on Fargo's head. "Because your parents live in a decent part of San Antonio and have friends and neighbors. If they came up missing, there'd be an outcry. The Rangers and the army and everybody else would be looking for them. These Germans just wanted to go about their work quietly after they watched your parents' house and figured out that much. So they tried to swipe Kristina off the stagecoach, and I just happened to show up in time to stop it. Then they made a deal with a Comanche band so they could grab you—"

Amid Greta's instant sobs, Fargo apologized, although he didn't see any way around mentioning that horror. "That's all I've managed to figure out," he interjected, hoping she'd quit weeping and resume talking. As he waited, he tried bending his head, so he could mop his sopping brow against his collar, but all that produced was a worse headache.

After a quaking minute, she spoke. "You have it, Skye. The most of it, anyway. In 1848 there was a famine across Europe. People rioted. The King of France was overthrown. Paul and Father made pamphlets and many speeches in our country. For a little moment, they thought they had won. There were popular assemblies to make the laws. The old aristocrats lost their power."

She took a deep breath, which must have required considerable effort, before continuing. "But it was all in vain. The armies of the kings crushed the people's hopes. Many of Father's friends were put in prison. Some were hanged. Many came to America. Germans had settled already in Texas, so we felt welcome here."

Was it just his imagination, or did those thongs feel looser? Wouldn't hurt to keep wiggling, and if he could keep Greta talking, then she wouldn't be crying. "That's all quite a ways in the past, Greta."

She heard something he didn't, likely because some little critters had to be taking drum lessons in his ears. "Hush, they are coming in," Greta advised.

Fargo sat straight with as much comfort as he could

summon. He didn't want to sit too rigidly, or his captors might think he was thinking, which invariably led to problems. Nor did he want to look relaxed, because then they'd check his bonds. He felt like he'd done a good job when the door opened.

Light flooded into the dark room, followed by two men, both in gray tunics that looked kind of military. Both were tall and squared off—even their impassive faces looked rectangular. They barked and grunted some guttural German before one turned to Fargo.

"Why is it that you pursue us, Herr Fargo? Is the Amerikaner army interested in us? Or perhaps these Rangers of Texas?"

Fargo shrugged.

"I asked you a question, *schweinhund*. Answer me."

The Trailsman shrugged again.

"Look, then, at the lady. See that on her chest. You wish one for yourself?"

Shrugging didn't seem like such a good idea anymore, but Fargo didn't know what else to do.

"Perhaps you would rather watch as we do that again to her. Would that help you find your tongue? Be assured, Herr Fargo, that we can find a way to make you talk. Think about that."

Fargo did think about it while the men made a cursory inspection and left. It was one thing to get branded yourself because you didn't talk. That was your problem. But to have to watch someone else suffer on your account was different. It wasn't like he had any secrets anyway. He figured he'd talk plenty when the time came, but there was no sense in rushing matters. Let those bastards think for a while that the army or the Rangers might be looking for them.

He flexed his wrists when the door shut behind them, and they seemed to move even better than before. His lake-blue eyes met Greta's.

"They do seem to want answers to a lot of questions, don't they?"

She nodded, grimacing because her own salty perspiration in this sweltering room was running down into her raw scar. "And all I know is that Paul went back because he is an engineer. In military school, he learned to make designs for forts and bridges. He wanted to build railroads here. But no one wanted to build a railroad in Texas. And he was offered such a wonderful position in the old country."

"So there's no politics involved?" Fargo wondered.

"I cannot say. Of course one hears of efforts to unite Germany in a democracy like America. But I don't know if Paul is part of those again. He seldom writes at all, and when he does, he says little. But those men . . ." She grimaced and bit her lip. "Those men won't believe me when I say that I don't know any more. Poor Kristina is with them now."

"How many men?"

"Four of them now. They are such brutes, Skye—"

"Just a minute," Fargo interposed. He wanted to focus on his hands. He could damn near move them. Why? Of course. Rawhide stretched when it got wet, and he was sweating enough so that it felt like a creek was flowing down his arms.

He forced his wrists apart, hating the way the thin cord cut into his skin. But if he kept worrying the rawhide bonds, he'd get them loose. It was just a question of time, and he might as well talk to pass the time. But suddenly there was the sound of approaching footsteps.

To make sure that the three men who entered got answers, they brought Kristina with them. She looked somewhat worse for the wear, but she hadn't been abused the way Greta had. The young woman stood straight, eyes closed and a gag in her mouth, with her hands lashed behind her. The man at her side, apparently the leader here, pushed her toward the stone wall under the window.

The other two men, the same pair that had come in earlier, took places beside Fargo and Greta.

As soon as he was sure he had everybody's attention, the leader grabbed the neckband of Kristina's dress and jerked. Cloth ripped all the way down to her waist. He released his grip and pointed to her quivering breasts.

"This woman is in no position to speak now," he hissed. "But you two can speak, am I correct?"

Both Fargo and Greta managed to mutter agreement.

"Good. Because we want very much to listen. Now, Herr Fargo, think hard upon why you worked so hard to find us. We want to know what traitors are paying you, and why. And Frau Baker, your brother, another traitor, must have mentioned his conspirators and his plans. We want you to tell us about that."

Like Greta, the Trailsman sat, his face an expressionless mask. His eyes flitted toward Kristina's full breasts. He admired the sight, although the circumstances were unpleasant. The guard standing at his left side wore a shiny black pistol belt, but the holster was on the other side.

After a silent eternity, the leader spoke again. "No answers, yet?" He sighed. "I feared as much." He grunted something loudly, and the door opened. The fourth man, shorter and darker than the others, stepped in. He held something with two wooden handles, each better than a foot long. From Fargo's vantage, the business end was an iron circle. He recognized the tool as a sharp-edged nipper, used for trimming horses' hooves.

Now, however, the leader held its biting end about two inches away from Kristina's right nipple. "The young lady has most excellent breasts, does she not?" A forced note of sadness entered his sinister voice. "It is a pity that I shall be compelled to deface her beauty unless your memory improves." He opened the nipper and pushed it slowly toward the erect nipple, which was shuddering like the rest of Kristina. Even though she was blindfolded, she had to have had a good idea of what was going on right in front of her.

While everyone looked that way, Fargo stretched his bonds again. Good. There was enough slack now to where he could slide the knot down so that his fingers could work on it. But not if anybody was watching him.

Fargo's eyes met Greta's, and she read his intentions.

Greta coughed a couple of times. They looked at her. "No, please, no," she shrieked hoarsely. "Paul is in Vienna."

"Ahh, so you do remember now." The leader smiled, turning toward Greta. "Who are his friends there in the Austrian capital?"

Greta scrunched up her face and began to intone names. Fargo recognized several of them as names he had seen on signs in front of shops, just down the road in Fredericksburg. But their captors seemed to think Greta was telling them something important, and as Greta rattled on, Fargo slipped his hands free, although he left them behind the chair.

Growing hoarser by the second, Greta paused to catch her breath. When she resumed, her voice was just a whisper. The man at Fargo's side leaned forward, just to be sure he wouldn't miss any names that would go on a secret-police list, to be rounded up and imprisoned over on the other side of the world.

The Trailsman, too, leaned forward, about as far as he thought that a man could if the man still had his hands tied behind the chair. His right arm moved down smoothly to his boot, and his hand inside. Except for the short guy who'd brought in the nippers and had stepped back to stand by the door, everybody was on the other side of the room. And he was trying to decide whether to stare at Kristina's bosom or listen to Greta's recitation of German names, along with occupations, like printer or mechanic.

Fargo's fingers were on the knife. It was out, mostly hidden under his palm. The razor edge nicked him as he applied it to the bond around his right leg, hoping that it would stay put. But it fluttered toward the floor, which caught the dark eyes of the short gent.

"*Achtung!*" he shouted, reaching for his pistol. He just cleared the holster when the flying knife plunged into his Adam's apple. Frothy blood, a torrent of pink bubbles, gushed from the hole in his throat. The man looked down through the spray. He couldn't see the handle, since it was under his protruding chin, and he had trouble locating the pistol in his own hand.

He tried to holler something else as he began to weave, but his vocal cords and windpipe had been sliced. When he attempted to speak, he just sprayed bubbles of blood. When he didn't, his lifeblood spouted in a steady pumping flow.

He rocked forward, sending a torrent of blood into the room. He slid a foot up, which gave him enough balance to topple backward as his red gusher arced toward the ceiling.

Fargo didn't watch much of that, though. He sprang up, standing for the first time in what seemed like hours. His own guard was going for a pistol, a notion the Trailsman discouraged with a roundhouse right to the man's temple. It slammed him toward Greta and the leader, getting him out of the Trailsman's way.

Spinning on his loose right foot, Fargo swung his left leg, chair still attached, at Greta's tall guard. Lunging for Fargo, with a chair smashed against his legs, the man swung one hand back, right into Greta's mouth. Maybe she was hungry, because she sure took a full bite.

Pain and anger flushed across his face. He turned, swinging at Greta with a fist while he tried to wrench his other hand free from her clenched teeth.

The Trailsman hobbled forward, getting his legs closer together beneath him. It was hard to keep from falling onto this plank floor, slippery with blood from the writhing man sprawled by the door who hadn't quite finished dying yet.

Fargo didn't get close enough in time to stop the man from slamming Greta's ear with his fist. He couldn't tell whether the brutal blow had knocked her unconscious, but he could see that it hadn't loosened her toothy grip on his now-bleeding hand.

The man's bent back was to Fargo. The Trailsman momentarily pondered a rabbit punch to the kidneys. But that was dirty fighting, and besides, why bother when it was so easy to reach ahead and come back with the man's pistol, slipping out of his spit-shined holster?

Its mechanism wasn't familiar to the Trailsman. He could have figured it out in a few seconds, but he didn't have a few seconds. Even at that, Fargo judged it would still function fine if used as a club. Grasping the pistol's twin six-inch barrels, he swung his arm around and high. The walnut-stocked butt smashed into the soft spot at the base of the man's skull, right at the top of his neck.

His head reflexively snapped back. Fargo felt a momentary twinge that he hadn't finished the job. But then the anguished but frozen face rolled on back, reaching an impossible angle. The man slumped to the floor, his eyes glazed over, as Greta opened her mouth and let the man finish falling.

The Trailsman turned. His first guard was getting up, pistol in hand. If the bastard had a gun, why hadn't he shot from the floor?

Because, Fargo discovered a moment later, he was covering for the leader, whose rear end could be seen through the open door, vanishing into the late-afternoon shadows on the dogtrot. Kristina was no longer in the room; he had taken her with him.

All Fargo had in hand was something that looked like a dueling pistol, and he could likely spit farther than it could shoot accurately. Not that he needed range right now, because the rising guard with the drawn gun wasn't more than a few steps away. Lumbering steps, if Fargo took them with a chair still tied to his left leg.

So Fargo flung the pistol with a sidearm cast and lunged toward the man's right side. No sense going straight, just in case the guard managed to pull that trigger. Moments after the thrown firearm smashed his nose, the German fired. The bullet flew harmlessly past Fargo, but Greta was still back there somewhere. And with that rock wall, the lead was still bouncing when Fargo sprang toward the reverberating cloud of powder smoke.

Somewhere inside it there had to be a man, but for an eyeblink, it seemed that the Trailsman was contending with a magician who knew how to conjure up a puff of smoke and vanish within it. Fargo's free foot went down hard as he clawed for the wall, hoping to keep himself up.

The resulting anguished cry told him that the guard had fallen. Maybe the thrown pistol had cost him his bearings, or he could have just slipped on the slaughter-slickened floor. But for whatever reason, the man had tumbled, and Fargo's boot heel had landed right on his balls with crushing force. The bastard was already yowling in soprano, a couple of octaves above his normal pitch.

And he wasn't quite out of it, yet. Even as he rolled himself up into a little ball when Fargo's foot came up, he pawed at the Trailsman's legs, raking Fargo's stitches with the pistol barrel, trying somehow to bring the Trailsman down.

His hands pressed against the wall to keep his balance, Fargo swung his chair-laden foot at the flailing body. The wooden legs snapped as they struck the men's head and neck. Despite his best efforts to stay up, Fargo tumbled sideways.

He scrambled to sit up, to get his hands before him for some protection. It was difficult because his chair leg was caught. He started to crab away, through a growing pool of blood, before he realized that the room was quiet. Ignoring the pain of a twisted leg, he turned to his sprawled opponent.

The shattered remnant of one chair leg was jammed deep into the socket of the man's right eye. His other blinked reflexively, wiping away some of the blood that poured across it. Not just blood. The sharp chunk of wood had penetrated so far that fragments of brain matter oozed at its splintered edges.

Fargo pushed himself that way with his hands, trying to untwist his leg. The more he tried, the more gore that emerged on the man's tormented face.

He turned his head toward Greta. She was shuddering, but alive. Fargo needed a knife so he could cut the chair free. But the only knife he knew about was across the room, stuck in a man's throat, and Greta was still tied down, unable to get it for him.

As a kid, the Trailsman had torn the wings and legs off captured flies a few times before deciding that watching creatures suffer wasn't anything he'd ever enjoy. So he didn't like what he had to do next, but then again, he hadn't asked for this in the first place. He hadn't been the one to lay hot iron on Greta and he hadn't hired any Comanche to torture her husband, one of Fargo's oldest friends.

Okay, perhaps the torture had been the Indians' idea, but swiping Greta from her family was entirely a German notion. Trying not to look, but knowing he had to, the Trailsman put his hands on the wall and shouldered upward. His weight shifted to the captured foot, sending the stub of a chair leg deeper into the man's brain. Fargo got his free foot under him and lifted the other. The man's head, then torso, came up with it. He had to shake it free.

Even though the floor had enough blood to soak his shirt, crawling over to the door was something of a relief. Fargo gulped in some fresh air, then fetched his knife from the short man's throat. He cut the chair off his left leg, then stood free and stretched before slicing Greta's bonds.

As he figured, the leader—Greta said his name was Albrecht Meyer—had ridden off with Kristina. No horses were in the corral; Meyer must have turned them loose. Fargo whistled for his Ovaro, then kicked in the door of the other side of the dogtrot.

Preferring to stay out in the fresh air and waning sunshine, Greta didn't go in with him. For a place where four men had been hiding out, it was surprisingly clean. But these men had seemed military, more or less, so that was understandable. In the top drawers of a bureau, he found his Colt, and his Sharps was stowed neatly in a closet, along with some other rifles. A leather sack in another drawer clanked, so Fargo opened it.

More coins. A lot of them, mostly silver talers, about the size of a silver dollar, although there were at least two dozen gold pieces, somewhat larger than American double-eagles. Carrying the bag, as well as his own gear, Fargo stepped out to find Greta on the edge of the dogtrot, holding the Ovaro's reins.

"What about Kristina, Skye?"

"Find her," Fargo said. "Though it's getting on dark and he's got a jump on us."

Greta pointed to the other horses, now standing idly at the edge of the clearing. "They must be riding double, as I count the horses."

"So he won't make time," Fargo agreed. He hurt worse than ever, and he couldn't recall ever feeling this tired. Even his bones creaked and protested at the idea of anything but a hot bath and a feather bed. But this wasn't the time to relax. "Let's go get her, then."

Aching steps took him to a shed by the corral, where he found the saddles and tack.

The tracks of the horse that carried Albrecht Meyer and Kristina Gottlieb led toward Fredericksburg. With the town in sight, Fargo reined up. How in thunder was the man going to get across a reasonably civilized town while riding double with a tied-up woman? Sure, folks tended to mind their own business, but not that much.

Well, if he'd been doing this, he'd lay over in some secluded woody spot until darkness. Then he'd head into town and find some shelter until he could round up some help or coax Kristina to talk or whatever. Thanks to the local habit of building Sunday houses, on any weekday there would be a plentitude of places to hole up in for a couple of days.

But Kristina knew more about Fredericksburg than Meyer did. And so he'd try to get her to talk. She'd likely mention the Bakers' Sunday house. Where Minerva was supposed to be waiting, out of sight of Clement Oakley, who was likely enjoying supper right now in the dining room at the Nimitz before taking an evening stroll.

Shit. He pulled out the clinking leather bag and turned to Greta. "Take this money. You might need it."

"Why, Skye?"

"I'll get to that. Ride over to your Sunday house. There's a woman in it named Minerva. She's an escaped slave. Tell her who you are—Kristina's sister—and that I sent you. And get her and you the hell out of there, pronto."

"Where do we go?"

"Anywhere you can get a room. Downtown is best. The more of a crowd around you, the safer you'll be. Folks thinking the way they do sometimes, you and Minerva might have trouble renting a room. But I want you to stay together, and I reckon there's enough gold in there to be damn persuasive."

She looked into the sack. "I could buy a house with this, Skye."

"You already own one, so don't do that unless you have to." He smiled. "Now, get going."

She kicked her mount and headed into town. Splattered with blood and riding astride, she would doubt-less cause some talk. But Fargo felt reasonably confident that Greta would get the job done.

He had his own work to do. From the wagon road, he turned off to follow the deep tracks from Meyer's double-ridden horse. After about half a mile, the land dipped into a brush-choked bottom along a creek, a good place to hide. And the creek flowed toward Fredericksburg, giving Meyer a concealed route into town.

By now it was full dark. There wasn't any sense charging into this spot. Lead could be flying every which way, or Meyer might just put a pistol to Kristina's ear and announce that he would kill her if the Trails-man came within sight. It would be better to wait elsewhere.

The overwhelming darkness, combined with some-thing close to utter exhaustion, made it a struggle for the Trailsman to stay awake during his vigil beside a privy on the outskirts of Fredericksburg, about twenty yards above the babbling creek. He wanted to visit it again. He'd washed his face and hands the first time, and now he could use that bracing tingle that came with a faceful of cold water.

Above the creek's sleep-inducing murmur, Fargo finally heard something moving. He padded down the hillside, down a narrow path doubtless used by local white-tailed deer. They didn't like to make any noise at night, either.

Next to a moss-draped oak just steps from the creek, he tensed. Atop the horse before him, two shapes blotted out stars. He sprang, grabbing the cantle to pull himself aboard.

For a horse that had to be awful tired of being ridden double, this one sure got frisky in a hurry. He either didn't want to even try toting three riders, or there was enough stink of fresh blood in Fargo's clothes to make him rambunctious.

The horse pitched forward and kicked up its rear heels. Meyer, sitting comfortably in the saddle with Kristina jammed before him, jerked the reins and sent a breath-stealing elbow back to the Trailsman's belly.

Fargo struggled to catch his breath as the horse found energy to spurt toward the center of Fredericksburg, pitching sideways and crow-hopping along the way. Without stirrups to help him stay aboard, the Trailsman needed both hands just to grip the cantle.

Some folks were still out in Fredericksburg to watch the show. In fact, there was a considerable crowd on the main street, right in front of the Nimitz Hotel. The coal-oil streetlights provided enough illumination for them to see the snorting horse pound toward them, then stop abruptly before the crowd, spilling Kristina down its neck.

Amid all that lurching, Fargo got an arm around Meyer's neck. He jerked back. Meyer reached down for his pistol. Fargo got his own out, but he'd barely cleared the holster when they both rose toward the stars, courtesy of the horse. The Trailsman continued bringing his Colt up inside this flying tangle.

Meyer seemed to have the same thing in mind, although it was too dark to be certain. What was certain was that the Trailsman's bullet caught him square in the chest. He was dead before he hit the ground.

Landing hard and in a heap, the Trailsman lay still amid the clamor and caught his breath before sitting up. He just felt too damn wore out to be shooting men in midair, in the dark like that. A hand appeared before him, and when he accepted the assistance and stood up, he saw it belonged to Clement Oakley.

Even worse, there were Minerva and Greta, kneeling at Kristina's side, maybe ten yards away. Kristina looked all right; she was sitting up and talking. But it was Oakley Fargo was worried about. Fargo had just been buying time when he'd agreed to find Minerva for her owner, thinking that he'd deal with the rest later.

But later was now.

Except Oakley was shaking his hand. "You are a marvel, Mr. Fargo. A true marvel."

Fargo felt more like an anvil after a long day of hammering, and his ears were even ringing that way. But he nodded. "If you say so."

"Not only do I find my runaway Minerva on your

account, Mr. Fargo, but that woman has already purchased the troublemaker from me for a considerable profit." He withdrew the handshake and reached into his pocket. A pouch with fifteen twenty-dollar gold pieces landed in Fargo's hand. "Here's the reward I promised for the fugitive. And thank you. I should be glad to treat you to dinner once you've had the opportunity to bathe."

Still dazed and not entirely sure of what was going on, the Trailsman ignored the crowd and shuffled toward Kristina, who was now standing, flanked by Greta and Minerva.

He looked at Greta. "I never figured you for a slave owner."

"I used his money." She pointed at Meyer's body. "And I am setting her free as soon as I can record the transaction at the court house. There is more than enough gold here to get her to Laredo and over the border to her husband."

She started to say more about her low opinion of slavery, but Fargo cut her off.

"Glad it worked out that way, Greta." He looked across all three women. "Reckon I'm due for a bath and some dinner, and some heavy-duty rest. See you gals in the morning." He tipped his hat and began to turn, but they started chattering, their voices low so that the dispersing crowd wouldn't hear them.

"Why don't you come to the Sunday house?" Greta suggested. "It's been years, Skye. Years."

"Mr. Fargo, I just know I could give you a bath that would heal you up good. Make you feel like a new man," Minerva advised.

"Look, Greta, just because you're my big sister, that doesn't mean you can hog all the good things in life," Kristina shot out. "And you, Minerva, you're not a free lady yet, you know."

As their discussion continued and got louder, Fargo turned and shuffled toward the hotel. Right now, he felt sure that he wanted to sleep, alone and unbothered, for about a week. But he also knew that after a bath and dinner, he'd likely wander over to the Sunday house, just to see if the women had settled their argument.

LOOKING FORWARD!

**The following is the opening
section from the next novel in the exciting
Trailsman series from Signet:**

THE TRAILSMAN # 87
BROTHEL BULLETS

---

*1860, the border country of the
Arizona territory west of
Chiricahua Peak, where law and
order were only words . . .*

The big man's hands went to the Colt on his hip, but
that was only an automatic reaction. He inclined his
head, ears straining. He almost hadn't heard the sound
at all in the rain that beat a soft but steady tattoo
against the forest leaves. It came again, somewhere
ahead of him, not a cry, not a sob, a kind of whimper.

His lake-blue eyes peered through the last of the
twilight. He wiped his face against the sleeve of his
rain slicker and moved his horse forward. A gust of
wind flung the rain into his face and he shook his head
just as the sound came once again, closer now. He slid
from the saddle and landed silently on the wet grass.

He moved forward on foot as the raindrops slid
down his face. He'd been riding slowly through the
steady rain for the past two hours, idly watching for a

place to bed down out of the rain, and now he pushed through a bank of tall, wet bushes and found himself in a small clearing. He wiped away the raindrops that dripped down from the top of his rain slicker and made out the small form in the last of the light. A frown came to his brow as he took in the slender girl, arms upraised, both wrists tied to the low branch of a tree. She wore only a dark-red dress, soaked through, plastered against a thin figure. Brown hair pressed half across a small, frightened face. He was beside her in two long-legged strides. "Jesus," Skye Fargo muttered. "What happened to you?"

"Help me," the girl half-sobbed as she peered up at him. She wasn't more than twelve or thirteen years old, he guessed. "He'll be back. Help me, please," she murmured.

"Who'll be back?" Fargo asked.

The voice cut into the girl's answer. "Mind your own business, mister," it said, and Fargo turned to see the man a few feet away through the curtain of rain.

"You leave her tied in the rain like this?" Fargo asked.

"I did. I'm her pa," the man said.

"He is not," the girl's voice cut in, suddenly stronger. "He's lying."

Fargo's eyes bored into the man and took in a thin face with a three-day stubble. "You're her pa and you left your daughter tied up like this in this downpour. She's soaked to the bone," he said.

The man took a step closer. "Only so she wouldn't run away again. That's all she does, run away," he said. "I went lookin' for a dry place."

"He's lying. Help me," the girl cried out, desperation in her voice.

"She already ran away once tonight. Took me hours to catch her," the man said.

"No, don't listen to him. I'm not his daughter. It's all lies," the girl said.

Fargo felt the frown crease his brow. He never liked becoming involved in family problems. You almost always ended up on the wrong side of everyone. The man's voice broke into his thoughts. "She's not right in the head, mister. She's been my problem ever since her ma died," he said. "You just leave her to me."

"He's making it all up," the girl shouted, and tried futilely to twist free of the branch.

Fargo felt the rain drop down across his narrowed eyes as he turned to the girl. "Keep your voice low," he said. "What's your name?"

"Katy," she murmured in a whisper.

He turned back to the man. "What's her name?" he asked.

"Katy," the man said, and Fargo's lips tightened. He let thoughts race through his mind again.

"Guess you do have a problem, mister," he said, and began to walk away.

"No," the girl screamed after him. "Help me. Don't listen to him."

"I'll take care of her," the man said reassuringly, and Fargo pushed through the tall bushes that slapped drops of water at him, found the Ovaro as the darkness closed down, and swung onto the horse. He rode noisily through the brush until he'd gone on a dozen yards, and then he reined to a halt. He slid from the horse again and dropped to the ground to move silently through the rain-soaked woods. The sound of the slap and the girl's sharp cry came to him as he neared the little clearing.

"Little bitch," the man's voice followed. "I don't care what Howie said. You're too goddamn much trouble. I'm not draggin' you back."

"You leave me alone," Fargo heard the girl say, defiance in her voice. The sound of another slap followed.

"Shut up," the man responded. "I'm gonna get me a little new pussy in the rain before I get rid of you."

Fargo moved forward with sudden speed, pushed his way through the brush, and stepped into the clearing. "You lied the first time around. I'll give you one more chance," he said, and saw the man spin around in surprise. The man stared at him, his face growing tight.

"You're real nosy, mister," the man growled. "Too nosy to stay alive."

Fargo saw the man go for his gun. He wasn't a very fast draw and his hand slipped for an instant on the wet butt of his six-gun. Fargo's hand, relatively dry inside his rain slicker, drew the Colt with one lightning-fast motion. The bullet tore through the bottom of the rain slicker and smashed into the man. His body made a watery thud as it hit the rain-soaked grass and he lay still, a dark circle instantly seeping onto the wet leaves.

Fargo stepped to the young girl, untied her wrist ropes, and caught her as she almost collapsed.

She clung to him, her slender, wet body shivering. "Thank you for coming back," she murmured. "Oh, God, thank you."

"We'll find some place dry, first. Then we talk," Fargo said. He kept his arm around her as he returned to the Ovaro. He lifted the girl onto the saddle and climbed on behind her. He sent the Ovaro forward another few hundred yards when a sudden burst of lightning illuminated the forest for a brief instant. But it was enough for him to glimpse the tall wall of earth and stone rising up on his left and he turned the horse toward it. He rode alongside the embankment, peering through the rainswept blackness. Another hundred yards on he spotted the half-circle of an extra deep blackness and watched it become the entrance to a cave.

Moving carefully, he nosed the horse into the mouth of the cave, listened, and drew in a deep breath. The cave was empty and he detected only the faint odor of marten and possum that had once tenanted it. The cave roof was high enough to hold the horse.

Fargo slid to the ground and lifted the slender, shivering form down with him. He left her leaning against the horse and groped his way around the floor of the cave to find enough pieces of wood to get a fire started. The girl sank to her knees in front of it at once.

"Get those wet clothes off," Fargo said. "I'll give you something dry to put on." He went to his saddle-bag, paused, and looked at her where she sat shivering, her eyes round on him. "Go on, dammit. You won't dry out with those wet clothes on," he barked.

She continued to hesitate, her brown eyes on him. She was really quite a pretty little thing when she didn't look half-drowned, he decided, soft, even features and wide, round eyes. "Go on, undress. I've seen bigger and better," he growled, and turned back to digging into the saddlebag.

When he pulled the flannel shirt out and turned to her, she was sitting naked, hands folded over a small black triangle and sweet, small breasts turning up that fitted the slender figure just passing into maturity. She took the shirt from him and disappeared inside it. He put another piece of dry wood on the fire and folded himself on the ground. "Talk to me. Start with your name," he said.

"Katy Hatchfeld," she said. "What's yours?"

"Fargo, Skye Fargo," he answered. "How'd he know your name was Katy?"

"He must've heard Althea call out to me," she said.

"Who's Althea?"

"My older sister. She's nineteen."

"How old are you?"

"Fourteen," she said with a touch of pride.

"How long have you been fourteen?"

"Three days."

"Tell me all of it, everything that happened," he said, and leaned back on one elbow.

Katy stretched her legs out to the fire. "I was coming back from Bisbee with Althea. My aunt lives there and she gave me a birthday party," the girl began. "Althea was driving our buggy with the roof, thank goodness. It started to rain real hard when suddenly these five men came out of nowhere and attacked us."

"Where's your sister now?" Fargo queried.

"They took her with them," Katy Hatchfeld said. "They're taking her to a whorehouse." She saw his brows lift and made an impatient face. "Yes, I know the word and I know what it is. That's why you've got to help me go after her."

"How do you know that's what they've done?" Fargo asked.

"They talked right about it."

"Why didn't they take you, too?" Fargo questioned.

"Their leader, a fat-faced idiot, said that Loveanne wouldn't want me and they could get more for me across the border," Katy said.

Fargo caught a certain note in her voice. "You sound disappointed. You feeling rejected?" he asked.

She tossed a glare back that suddenly softened. "Never thought about it that way," she murmured. "Maybe I did, sort of. Mostly I wanted to stay with Althea. But they just took her and left that other one to take care of me. Now we've got to go after Althea."

"We?" Fargo frowned.

"You'll be paid well for it. Our father is Owen Hatchfeld."

"Doesn't mean anything to me, doll."

"Well, he's rich and powerful up north of here in Mesa Springs. You know where that is?" Katy said.

"Been through it."

"My father will pay you whatever you ask if you save Althea."

"I think I ought to bring you to your pa," Fargo contemplated aloud.

"No! He's a day's ride north. You've got to get Althea first, before anything happens to her. God knows what they've got planned for her," Katy insisted.

"I've a pretty good idea what they've got planned for her," Fargo said grimly. "You remember anything else that could help?"

Katy's small face darkened in thought. "One of them mentioned a town. I'll think of it," she said, her brow furrowed in concentration when a burst of sudden excitement swept the furrow away. "Cactus Corners, that was the name," she exploded. "Yes, that was it."

"That's at least a half-day's ride from here," Fargo said.

"I know, Father does business there sometimes. I've heard him talk about it," the girl said. "Will you go after Althea?"

"I'll think on it," Fargo answered.

"I'll go alone if you won't come."

"That's really dumb."

"Althea needs help. Maybe I can find a way. I'd rather be dumb than afraid."

Fargo smiled. "I'll bet you're a real brat most of the time," he said.

She met his eyes with her chin lifted in defiance. "Maybe," she said. "But that makes no difference. Althea needs help, that's all that matters."

"Nobody's going anywhere till this rainstorm stops. Your clothes ought to be dry by then," Fargo said.

"Does that mean you'll go with me?" Katy asked, hope instant in her eyes.

"It means what I said. I'll think on it," he muttered. He stretched out beside the small fire.

Katy settled herself inside his shirt with a half-pout and Fargo closed his eyes. He had just finished scouting a trail from the Utah border to Nogales for Sid Allman, but Sid wouldn't be expecting him back for another few weeks. The girl needed help, that was plain enough. It was equally plain that he'd no good reason not to give it to her, except for maybe putting his ass in a sling, and he'd never let that stop him before. He snapped off further thoughts, let himself half-doze, and woke when he heard the rain begin to taper off. He sat up and saw Katy come awake, sitting with her head bowed, arms encircling her knees. "Your things dry yet?" he asked.

She reached over and felt the half-slip and dress. "Yes." She nodded.

He rose and walked to the mouth of the cave. The rain had stopped and the air was now thick and humid under the fast-moving clouds. The moon was beyond the horizon line and dawn was near. He listened and heard only the rainwater still dripping off the forest leaves. Turning back to the cave where the fire was now only a few burning embers, he saw Katy had dressed and held his shirt out to him.

"Thanks," she said. "You done with your thinking?" she added with a touch of asperity.

"Yep," he said flatly, and saw exasperation touch her young face.

"Well, dammit?" the girl snapped.

"I'll see about your sister, brat," he said.

The girl flew into his arms in an explosion of relief. "Thank you," Katy Hatchfeld said. "It'll be worth your while. Daddy'll see to that, believe me."

He pushed her back and his lake-blue eyes were agate-hard. "That didn't go into my deciding," he growled.

Katy blinked. "I'm sorry," she said, the apology real in her eyes and her voice. "Guess we've been brought up thinking too much about the importance of money."

"Guess it happens when you've too much of it," Fargo said, and her hands curled around his.

"Guess so. I didn't mean anything wrong," she said contritely, and he let his eyes soften.

"Bring my horse over," he said, and stepped out of the cave to see the first gray tint of dawn touch the sky. "What happened to the buggy you and Althea were riding?" he asked as she appeared with the Ovaro.

"I don't know. They just pulled us out and made off. I guess they left it," Katy said.

He climbed onto the horse and drew her up in front of him. "Can you remember where this happened?" he asked.

"West of here. We were on a road that ran alongside the heavy forest," Katy said.

"I think I know the one. Let's go have a look." He sent the horse west through the woods at a trot, skirted trees, and held the pace through the hours as the dawn broke fully, a gray sky at first and then the sun finally coming out. When he reached the narrow road that curved alongside the thick forest land, he peered down at the carriage tracks that were clear in the still-soft earth. He turned the Ovaro and followed the twin ruts, pointed out where the wheels had veered from one side of the road to the other.

"The horse was moving along by himself, nobody reining him in. They took Althea and left the buggy," Fargo said as they continued to follow the tracks. It was almost an hour before he spotted the horse and buggy just off the road, the horse grazing on a bed of grama grass. Fargo reined up and dismounted beside the buggy. As Katy watched, he unhitched the horse, put a blanket over him as the Indians did, and motioned to the girl. "We'll make better time with you riding your own mount," he said as she pulled herself onto the horse.

"Is that the only reason?" she asked.

"You're too young to be that suspicious," Fargo muttered.

"I don't want you to think of sending me home alone," she said. "I want to help get Althea."

He fastened her with a stern glance. "You'll do whatever I think best, or I quit right now," he growled.

She glowered back for a moment but finally nodded. "All right," she murmured, and brought the horse in beside him.

"Ride," he told her, and turned the Ovaro northward, staying on the road for another half-hour. He then cut into the wooded terrain again. Katy rode in silence beside him as his eyes scanned the forest. He made no attempt to pick up tracks, not after the heavy rain. Besides, the kidnappers could have gone a very different route. It was past noon when they emerged from the woods and he saw a road and, traveling slowly along it, a cut-under buggy with a hardtop roof and elliptical springs.

He veered the Ovaro to the left and cut across the buggy's path to see two young women in the carriage, both in their early twenties, both dark-haired, attractive, and well-dressed. He reined to a halt. "Good day, ladies." He smiled. "You know the country around here?"

"I'm afraid not," the young woman driving replied. "We're just passing through on our way to San Xavier."

"Mighty rugged country for two young ladies to be traveling through alone," Fargo remarked.

"We're careful," the girl answered.

"And prepared," the other one said, and lifted an old Remington rifle from the floor.

"Glad to see that." Fargo smiled.

"We'd be at San Xavier by now if it hadn't been for that storm last night. We turned back and spent the night with a friend," the driver said.

" 'Fraid we were caught in it, too," Fargo said. "Good luck on your way," he added with a nod, and sent the Ovaro into a trot across the road and into the flat land on the other side.

"I guess Althea and I should've been more prepared," Katy said as she rode beside him. "But they came onto us so suddenly it wouldn't have mattered much."

"Maybe not," he agreed.

They rode toward a line of low hills in the distance. The sun had reached the midafternoon sky when they crossed the first hill and saw a lone house on the next rise in the land.

"Let's go ask some questions," Fargo said.

The house had a front yard with six big Tamsworth hogs in it, and a broad-faced woman came to the door. "Afternoon, ma'am," Fargo called out pleasantly. "You happen to see four men and a girl come this way?"

"No," the woman answered.

"They'd have been heading for Cactus Corners," Fargo mentioned.

"Then they'd likely have taken the back side of that hill," she said, and nodded to a low hillside beyond. "There's a road that comes close to Cactus Corners after a few hours' riding."

"Good enough," Fargo said. "Might you know of a decent place to stay in Cactus Corners?"

"In that hellhole of a town?" the woman flung out.

"Ellie Bensen's boardinghouse would be the only place. That town's a kettle of sin."

"Is that so?" Fargo said mildly.

"It's made of whorin', boozin', and thievin'. Every no-good, rotten scheme in the country finds a place to hatch there. The only decent folks are those who have to work and live there, and I feel sorry for them," the woman said. Her eyes went to Katy. "It's no place for a young girl like her," she sniffed.

"We won't be staying long." Fargo smiled. "Much obliged for your advice." He tipped his hat and moved the pinto forward at a walk.

Katy waited for the woman to go back inside the house before exploding the question. "Why'd you ask about a boardinghouse? You're not leaving me holed up someplace. I told you I wanted to help get Althea," she snapped.

"Damn, you're a pain in the ass, girl," Fargo rasped. "You'll get your chance to help. First I have to do some snooping around without worrying about you."

Katy accepted the answer but her glower stayed.

They rode over the hill the woman had pointed out and found the road on the other side. When he took the road north, his eyes scanned the hoofprints he came upon and lifted to survey the land alongside the road.

"See anything?" Katy asked after an hour's riding.

"Maybe. There were a few clusters of prints but nothing clear enough for being sure," Fargo said. "I see too damn many Apache pony prints, though." He raised his eyes to the low hills nearby and the sandstone rock formations that rose up, some almost white, others a light red, all with more than enough towers and pinnacles to hide behind. He veered from the road when he spotted a small pool glistening under the late-afternoon sun. They halted to let the horses drink and to fill Fargo's canteen. He glanced at Katy and saw the tension in her face. "Getting worried?" he asked not ungently.

"Yes," she said. "Maybe we'll be too late."

"Maybe not," Fargo said. "I'm thinking they holed up out of the rainstorm last night. That'd mean they won't have reached Cactus Corners till sometime around midday today."

The girl drew a deep sigh and her small face tried to find hope. She climbed onto the horse and followed Fargo as he set off again, returning to the road until it began to veer left. He rode north across sandy terrain marked by tall saguaro cactus and a variety of smaller species. He took in the bright-red flowers of mound cactus, clusters of agave and echeveria, and plenty of the rounded fishhook cactus with their slender outer spines. He heard Katy bring her horse closer as a grunt escaped his lips.

"What is it?" she asked.

"They came along this way," Fargo said. "That cluster of hoofprints there, at least four or five horses." He halted, dismounted, and ran his fingers over the hoofprints. "Not more than three or four hours old," he said, and returned to the pinto.

"You're real good at this," Katy remarked.

"I'm a trailsman," he said. "You got lucky."

"Yes, it seems so," the girl agreed, and hurried her horse to catch up to him as he put the magnificent black-and-white Ovaro into a fast canter.

The last of the day faded into dusk and the darkness came quickly and they were still riding. It was well into the night when he glimpsed the dark outlines of buildings to the right and made for them.

The town was bustling as late as it was when they reached it. He slowed to a walk. There were plenty of men on the main street and a good sprinkling of Texas top-bow wagons. He heard the sound of the dance hall before they reached it, a tinny piano drifting out into the darkness and the murmur of boisterous voices. He slowed when he came into sight of the big building, larger than he'd expected. Wide double doors fronted the building and he read the large sign that hung over the entrance:

THE CACTUS KITTEN
Dancing, Drinking, & Dallying

"This has to be it," he heard Katy murmur.

"Just ride on by," Fargo said as three men half-fell, half-walked out of the place. He rode on a few yards farther before he turned sharply, cut through a narrow space between two buildings, and came out at the back of the town. He moved along until he had retraced his way to the rear of the brothel, and his eyes were narrowed as he scanned the building. Long, with two stories to it, it had two back doors. His eyes went to the second floor, where a long row of windows looked down, most curtained and half softly glowing with candlelight.

A smooth sumac grew some dozen yards away from the rear of the building. Fargo pointed to it. "Put that tree in your mind," he said.

Katy nodded and followed him as he rode on, cut between houses again, and returned to the main street. Once again he rode slowly past the front of the brothel. "Come two o'clock in the morning, you'll ride back here and find my Ovaro tied to the hitching post," he said.

"Where'll I be till then?" Katy asked.

"Out of sight in Ellie Bensen's boardinghouse," Fargo said.

"Where'll you be?" she asked.

"Inside the Cactus Kitten, trying to see if I can find Althea. It'll take time. I'll have to be real cagey," he said. "When you come back, unhitch my Ovaro and go wait with both horses under that sumac at the back. When I come out, you come running with the horses."

"I understand," Katy said soberly. "What if you don't find Althea?"

"We worry about that later. You just be there," he said, as he reined up outside a trim house near the other end of town with the modest sign *Boarders* outside the door. A tall, gray-haired woman came to the door when he knocked, her face thin and edging severeness. "I'd like a room for my little sister for the night," he said, and the woman's glance took in Katy with quick appraisal.

"We can do that," the woman said. "Just sign the register, please."

Fargo stepped into a neat, wallpapered hallway where a ledger rested on a wall shelf. He saw the tall grandfather clock in one corner and nodded to it, and Katy answered with her eyes.

"See you tomorrow, honey," Fargo said with brotherly concern as she followed the woman down the hall. He hurried from the boardinghouse, swung onto the Ovaro, and headed back to the brothel. When he reached it, he tethered the Ovaro to the end of the hitching post and walked up two steps to push through the wide double doors. The clock at the boardinghouse had said eleven. That gave him three hours to find Althea, if she was there. It was enough time if he played it right. Enough time to get himself killed trying, he added grimly.